Critics applaud STRANGLED PROSE, the first Claire Malloy Mystery

"The narrator's tone is flippant, relishing the antics in academe. A divertissement!"

Newsday

"A snappy novel about the murder of a romance writer . . . Entertaining."

Chicago Sun-Times

"The author's style is conversational and airy, full of rue and wry."

The Kirkus Reviews

"Frothy entertainment."

Library Journal

STRANGLED PROSE

Joan Hess

BALLANTINE BOOKS • NEW YORK

 Published in the United States of America by Ballantine Books, a division of Random House, Inc., New York, and simultaneously in Canada by Random House of Canada Limited, Toronto.

Library of Congress Catalog Card Number: 85-25146

ISBN 0-345-34059-0

This edition published by arrangement with St. Martin's Press

Manufactured in the United States of America

First Ballantine Books Edition: February 1987

For my parents, with love and respect

ONE

There is no place for a body in the little office at the back of my bookstore—not even mine. With a concerted effort and a great deal of grunting and shoving, I had managed to squeeze in a small wooden desk, two chairs, and a dented filing cabinet with two drawers. That left very little floor space, but it did give me a place to pretend to do the necessary managerial duties. I love books; I hate bookkeeping—except in a whimsical sense.

The Book Depot is in a renovated train depot; hence, the uninspired but accurate name. The red brick building was the focal point of the town until the late 1940s, when the last passenger train rumbled into the sunset. After that it was used by the railway agents who dealt with occasional freight trains. Those, too, finally found another route, and the building was abandoned.

A white-haired elf named Grimaldi bought the building when the final train withered on the track. He spent what money he had for remodeling, then ordered the inventory, put up his sign, and promptly fell dead with a stroke. Mrs. Grimaldi sold me the store on her way to Florida.

Now it is mine, and like a marriage, the relationship is not dependable. But I love the musty corners, the flaking plaster, and the memories of a happier time. I have always known that I ought to own a bookstore, if only to have access to a satisfactory source of books. The cramped office goes with the job; it must have provided some comfort to the shivering agent, since the boiler rarely did. The boiler is still with me, but I have contemplated a divorce.

I was sitting in said office, surrounded by ledgers and stacks of invoices as I tried to arrive at a quarterly tax estimate that would fall somewhere between despair and credibility. When the bell above the front door tinkled, I abandoned the grim figures and went to the front of the store.

Mildred Twiller hesitated in the doorway, twisting a bit of Irish lace in her hand. "Claire, I need to speak to you—if you're not too busy?" Her voice tinkled like the bell above her head, delicate yet impossible to ignore.

I studied her nervously. Mildred reminds me of a snowman made of marshmallows, superficially soft but with a core of ice. She is short and sweet, with small, round eyes and a ladylike mouth carefully outlined in red. Two patches of pink had been brushed onto her alabaster cheeks. She was wearing a fluttery linen dress that murmured money to those who listened to such things, a large-brimmed hat, and her signature, a collection of bright silk scarves. She looked as if she were a silver-haired gypsy with a hefty income.

"Wonderful," I said, despising my weakness for the woman. She and I are from different worlds, but I like her. I brushed a layer of dust off my faded jeans and said, "Come on back to the office and we'll have coffee while we talk."

"I really don't want to interrupt you," she said in a self-deprecatory voice. "You must be terribly busy. I simply wanted to let you know that my newest book will be out in a few weeks." She resisted an urge to pirouette, but I could see the inner struggle.

"No, I can use a break, Mildred. The coffee is already made. Come on back and sit down for a minute."

We went to the office. Mildred looked at the chair uneasily, no doubt wondering if there was a tactful way to dust it with her handkerchief. I poured the coffee, handed her a mug, and perched on the corner of the desk. Like Macbeth, I sensed trouble.

"I was hoping you might have a little reception when the book arrives," Mildred chirped. Her eyes bored into me in silent command. "I'll supply the refreshments, naturally, and the invitations. I simply don't think it quite nice for me to have a party honoring me. People might think I was being a teensy boastful."

I pretended to consider it for a minute, then shook my head in a show of regret, which I felt not one little bit. "I'd love to host the reception, Mildred, but I really don't have enough room for a horde of people. Why don't you have the reception on campus? That way, no one will have to be left out, and—"

"I've always felt it vital to help my friends," Mildred cut in, as if I hadn't been so rude as to contradict her plan. "It's clear to Douglas and me that your little store isn't doing very well these days. We feel responsible for you, dear, and I am willing to limit my guest list to allow for the available space in order to help you."

"How will your reception help me?" I said in a

reasonable voice. Not that Mildred had ever been swayed by reason. In her unassuming way, the woman could withstand a hurricane or an earthquake. I told myself that I had better start thinking about rearranging the book racks in the front of the store.

"Everyone will attend the reception. A bookstore must have customers, and this will give people a chance to see how charming the Book Depot is. It will help quite a bit."

"I don't handle romance fiction," I said, in what I knew was a futile attempt to avert the inevitable. Custer waving at the Indians. Ahab reading a blubber recipe. "Your fans won't find much to interest them here. Now, the bookstore at the mall carries a lot of romance books, and they might be willing to—"

"Nonsense. My fans read other genres. Besides, Douglas will wish to invite many of the Farber faculty members. My book is entitled *Professor of Passion,* which will appeal to them. It takes place in a college setting."

"I'm sure it's quite wonderful, Mildred, but I don't think—"

"A Sunday afternoon would be preferable," she said. She dug through her leather purse and pulled out an appointment book. After glancing through it, she beamed at me. "Yes, November tenth would seem the most likely choice for the autograph party. From two to four, with champagne and a few things to eat."

"November tenth," I repeated numbly, "with champagne and autographs. What shall I do, Mildred?"

"Not a teensy thing. I'll have the caterer drop by in the next week or two to study the possibilities. All you'll need to do is decide where you want the various tables to be placed. I will need a certain amount of space to display and autograph my book."

"Are you sure it'll be out on schedule? I'd hate to plan—"

"My editor has assured me that the book will be available as scheduled, Claire." Mildred stood up and adjusted her hat to a rakish angle. "Just think of it as an opening night on Broadway."

Leaving me to ponder the image, Mildred Twiller swept out of the office. Seconds later, the bell tinkled and I was alone again. I leaned back in the chair to study the cracks in the ceiling. Where had I lost control of the situation with Mildred?

The problem is that the woman has the continuity of a schizophrenic. On one hand, Mildred is a rotund little grandmother who exudes the aroma of talcum powder and violets. But when she slips into the role of Azalea Twilight, a successful romance writer whose descriptive scenes leave even the most ardent pornographiles speechless with admiration, the woman grows taller. Her eyes begin to snap, her voice to crackle, and her vocabulary to pop with self-assurance. She's as irresistible as one of her virginal heroines.

After a few scowls at the ceiling, I dove back into the ledger to see if the figures had improved in my absence. My fairy godmother had failed to work on them, and they still looked a shade gaunt. Although my income rarely delights my accountant, my daughter, Caron, and I manage to manage. I am incredibly happy with the store, moderately happy with my drafty old apartment, and somewhat happy with Caron—when she's behaving like a human being rather than a pubescent tragedy. Fourteen is a difficult age. Caron has turned it into a well-staged melodrama.

At this point, I almost allowed myself to hunt up the latest adolescent psychology book to see if Caron's symptoms might be terminal. But indulging in a book is my worst fault, since I have been known not to surface for hours. With a martyred sigh, I returned to the accounts.

The bell tinkled again. I crammed the ledger in a drawer, ran a hand through my hair, and went to the front of the store, wondering if Mildred's caterer had arrived to rip out my shelves and put in a champagne fountain.

Britton Blake was studying the display of the current bestsellers. His bearded chin bobbled wisely and his hands were entwined behind his back. His arms formed a perfect vee, as in *valiant, versifier,* or *vasectomy*. All virtues, according to one's perspective.

He swung around to smile at me, confident that the leather patches were affixed firmly to the elbows of his tweed jacket and that his pipe would not tumble out of his pocket to disgrace him. It was one of my secret dreams.

"Claire, darling." He came at me, lips puckered hopefully.

I retreated down the aisle. "Hello, Britton. Browsing or buying?"

"If only your heart were for sale . . ." he began, in his most pedantic tone. "Dear Claire, 'she will show us her shoulder, her bosom, her face; but what the heart's like, we must guess.' Earl of Lytton, 1831–1891."

"Don't get your hopes up about the 'bosom' bit," I retorted, still edging backward. "My accountant assures me that the IRS will slap a lien on said bosom if I don't send in a quarterly estimate. So, feel free to browse, and leave the money on the counter if you find anything to buy—for a change."

Now the maligned schoolboy, Britton put his hand on his heart. "I came by with the most honorable of intentions. The student film society is showing a delightful little

Bergman film Sunday evening, and I thought we might have a bite of supper afterward."

"In the corner bistro? Farberville rolls up the sidewalk at ten o'clock, earlier when the Farber students have been exposed to something as risqué as a foreign film. Farberville can deal with X-rated movies, but films—ha!"

"Your logic is unassailable, as always. Since there is no bistro for a late supper, we can retire to my lodgings for a nibble or two." His leer was laden with suggestion.

Britton is certainly not the worst available man in town. He's divorced, but he doesn't have a flock of surly children who teethed on Cinderella's stepmother, nor does he bother with the nubile sorority girls. Although he spews a lot of nonsense, he's at least gentlemanly in his forthright and lecherous quest. Once in a while, my animal instincts have overcome my reluctance, and we've indulged in a bit of amorous frivolity.

To my regret, Britton takes the whole thing much more seriously than I do. I have the store, my daughter, and a reasonable future as a single woman. I tried men once. It was not an untenable arrangement, but when Carlton terminated the relationship in a car wreck, I vowed not to find a replacement. Prose filled the gap admirably. Britton refuses to believe me.

"Well?" He was pursuing me down the aisle, graphically as well as metaphorically. No doubt he was hearing an organ drone the familiar processional march.

"A Bergman film might serve to erase the scars," I admitted. I allowed him to tickle my cheek with his well-clipped beard, then distracted him with the story of Azalea Twilight's newest literary accomplishment.

"*Professor of Passion?* Good God, the woman should be locked in a library for the next decade to discover the essential truth of literature!" Britton's normally blue eyes were now circles of slate. "Have you actually read any of her—and I use the word in the loosest sense—work?"

We went into the office. After I handed him coffee, I sat down behind the desk. "I did read a couple, since Caron has every last one of them. What amazes me is that sweet little Mildred Twiller has such unbelievable fantasies. I don't believe people can actually do some of the contortions she describes in loving detail, much less enjoy it at the same time. She knows more erogenous zones than I do time zones."

"The underlying question is: Can you by any stretch of the imagination see Mildred and Douglas engaged in her pet erotica? Even in the name of literary research, I fail to find Mildred quite that inspirational."

"Under Mildred's floppy hat lies one of the most creative brains in the category fiction market. She has told me that when nearing one of her 'sensual scenes,' she opens a bottle of wine, surrounds her typewriter with candles and roses, and just lets herself flow with the sexual tide. The image boggles the mind."

Britton gave me an innocent smile. "Why don't we try out some of Mildred's ideas, simply to prove the impossibility of having one's tongue in more than two or three places at thc same time? Then, if we arrive at any conclusions, I can publish a scholarly article refuting her more descriptive passages."

"I can see the article in *Literary Dialogue,*" I said, nodding soberly. "You could title it 'An Exploration of the Erotic Premise of Anatomically Improbable Coitus in the Later Works of Azalea Twilight.'"

Britton glanced at his watch, then stood up and realigned the creases in his pants. "As distasteful as it seems, my graduate seminar on Elizabethan poetry requires my immediate attention. Shall we begin the research this evening? I'll stock up on aphrodisiacs, in case you find yourself unable to meet the challenge of behaving like Azalea's giddy heroines."

"Bergman is okay, but don't buy any powdered rhinoceros horns for me. Caron is having Inez over to study, and I dare not leave them alone for more than a few hours."

"Have they been reading Azalea Twilight's how-to manuals?"

"Manically, night and day. Between the two of them, they have two complete sets. They have memorized some of the more significant passages and sit around the living room quoting to each other. It unsettles me, at the very least."

Britton made a few more lazy attempts to corner me, then left to take out his frustrations on the hapless graduate students waiting in the English building. I stood in the doorway and watched him walk the few blocks up the hill to the campus. When he was out of sight, I shifted my attention to the Farber students crowding the sidewalk in front of my bookstore.

I reminded myself sternly that more than fifteen years had slithered by since I was an undergraduate. Although at thirty-eight one is supposed to embrace more conservative ideals, I rather wish the current students might show some faint flicker of spirit. It is only an idle dream. We had the Vietnam war to bring us together; they have only the threat of unemployment. The nightmare of not being able to afford designer clothes and designer houses keeps them in line. Farber students protest the dearth of fall interviews with prospective employers. Nuclear bombs and third-world famine leave them cold.

Enough of the soapbox. Of the six thousand students at

Farber, maybe one will turn out to be a leader of the underprivileged, a spokesman for equality, a champion of civil rights. After all, they can't all find jobs as advertising executives and philosophy instructors. Farber is a provincial liberal arts college; the recruiters have been known to ignore it during lean years.

I spotted a familiar figure jogging down the hill, holding a steady path in the middle of the sidewalk, despite the crowd. Nary a student would dare impede the progress of Douglas Twiller, M.A., Ph.D., holder of the Thurber Farber Chair of Literature, etc., etc. Not to mention husband of Azalea Twilight, which he actually didn't mention too often. Of course, his wife's books pulled in well over a hundred grand a year, by no means literary peanuts. They paid for the Mercedes, the servants, the mansion to keep the servants busy, and Douglas Twiller's designer jogging shoes. It would be churlish to belittle the typewriter that lays the golden egg.

Douglas swung into the store without losing a beat. Bouncing from foot to foot like a child in need of a potty, he gave me a broad wink. "Hi, Claire."

I regarded him with the same wariness I do his wife. Douglas is a virile specimen for his fifty-odd years. He has a trim beard, modestly long hair flecked with gray, a hard body, and a boyish grin. Quite a combination for an English professor, as his distaff students are inclined to giggle in the sanctity of the sorority houses. He insists on teaching at least one undergraduate course every semester, claiming that it helps him keep his teaching skills honed. Campus gossip attributes other motives.

"Hello, Douglas. Would you please stop hopping about like that? It ages me to see all that perfectly good energy being wasted."

"I can think of other ways to expend energy, Claire."

"I'm sure you can; please do not elaborate on the theme." I crossed my arms and waited.

His feet came to a reluctant halt. "Did Mildred come by this morning? She was eager to speak to you."

"Yes, she did. I think it's a truly wretched idea, but she did not agree. The Book Depot does not cater to literary voyeurs, and I have no desire to have my store filled with drooling—"

"Now, now, Claire." Douglas waggled a manicured finger at me. "Mildred and I consider you one of our dearest friends. Mildred is determined to help you, at whatever cost to her personally. I hope you won't do something that might cause her pain."

The man had unerring aim. I made a face and said, "I suppose not, Douglas. But this is the only time the Book Depot is going to engage in such a travesty. Make that clear to Mildred."

"To Mildred, yes. To Azalea Twilight, who knows?" He started the sneakers pounding, gave me a quick wink, and jogged out the door. A huddle of students leaped out of his way as he started back up the hill toward the campus. The Douglas Twillers of the world teach classes in sweat suits, drink jug wine at student parties, and generally break every written and unwritten rule of conduct. But, as their deans know very well, they do publish often in prestigious journals. And that's what matters.

The students came into the store, and I forgot about the reception as I helped them find the books on their starchy, crisp reading lists. Douglas, Britton, and several other of the English faculty feel some misguided obligation to take care of their departed colleague's widow, even after eight years. I would object—if I had a more reliable source of income. But you can't buy wine with food stamps, so I accept the business as graciously as possible.

I dealt with the students, even managing to sell one of them a book that was not on his reading list. A triumph, I crowed silently as I returned to the ledger.

At seven o'clock, I closed the store and walked up the hill. Caron and I have the top floor of an old house that sits across the street from Farber College's most famous landmark, Farber Hall. Although the health inspector condemns it on a semiannual basis, it still houses the English department and two floors of damp, cold classrooms. Carlton's office was on the fourth floor, and he used to joke about the building collapsing under his feet. He should have worried a little more about chicken trucks and icy pavement.

I checked the mail and eased open the front door. The ground floor was inhabited by yet another member of the English faculty. I had had enough contact with the group for the day, but apparently the gods were having a dull time on Olympus.

"Claire!"

I stopped, one foot dangling above the step, and turned around reluctantly to meet two militant eyes under a cap of black, cropped hair. She wore a khaki army jacket, baggy pants, and a T-shirt with a message about the role of men in today's society. It was obscene.

"What's up, Maggie?" I asked.

"Is it true?" If words had physical substance, hers would have splintered into a thousand shards.

"Is what true, Maggie?"

"Is it true that the Book Depot is sponsoring a reception for Azalea Twilight's newest bit of sexist garbage?"

"In a manner of speaking, yes. Mildred didn't phrase it quite like that, however."

Maggie's nose turned red and she began to huff. When it became clear that she was incapable of verbalizing her displeasure, I added, "If you're planning to ultimately blow the house down, I'd appreciate a chance to move out a few of my cherished possessions, and perhaps my daughter."

Maggie Holland is the president of the Farber Women's Organization, which periodically issues statements condemning whatever offends them. They picket once in a while, their beety faces shining with indignation and their arms locked in sisterhood. I approve of their sentiments, although they have been known to be a shade tedious in their demands. I don't want to play football, nor do I feel equality extends to urinals in the ladies' room.

At last Maggie found her voice. "I must say that I am appalled at you, Claire Malloy! You are aware that romance fiction proliferates the sexist tenet that a woman's single goal in life is to attach herself like a leech to some arrogant bastard who—"

"I'm doing a favor for Mildred," I said firmly. "If you don't approve of the book, make your statement clear by not attending the reception. Stay home and sulk. Read a pamphlet. Refuse to wash the dishes for the next month."

Maggie's mouth tightened, and her fingers dug into the doorjamb until I could almost feel them. "As leader of the FWO, I cannot overlook this, Claire. We have a moral obligation to eradicate this vile literature."

"I'm not sure the FWO has that kind of impact on the New York publishing houses, Maggie," I said. I started back up the stairs, tired of the whole thing.

"We're going to demonstrate!" Maggie yelped.

"So demonstrate!" I yelped back, without stopping. I

went upstairs, unlocked the door, then slammed it several times and stomped across the living room. Maybe Maggie's light fixture will fall on her head, I hissed to myself. I barely stopped myself from slamming the refrigerator door closed.

Caron's head popped up from behind it. Waving a half-eaten carrot at me, she said, "Mother, if you engage in coitus interruptus, are you still technically a virgin?"

And that was only the beginning.

TWO

October passed in a flutter of dried leaves and staggering football fans. I was still trying to force a glimmer of hope from the accounts. My accountant, a perfect model for Poe's raven, was amusing himself by hissing threats over the telephone. He refuses to come by the shop, swearing that his sports car would be endangered if he parked anywhere on the street. He has a valid point.

When the telephone shrilled at me, I presumed the dear man was calling once more to reiterate the IRS position on delinquent quarterly statements. I held the receiver several inches from my ear and muttered a faint, "Hello?"

"Claire, I need you for lunch today." Mildred, or Azalea. I couldn't be sure.

"What's the matter—out of frozen quiche?"

Clearly it was Mildred who said, "I thought we might have a nice shrimp salad, but if you'd prefer . . . ?" Pure bewilderment is always Mildred.

"Shrimp salad would be fine if I had the time, Mildred, but I don't. I'm going to schedule a bankruptcy hearing at two and then hit every bar on the street. I won't be sober until Friday at the earliest," I said, glaring at the ledger. Not funny, I lectured myself.

Mildred agreed with my silent assessment. "Now, Claire, everyone has to eat lunch. Hang a cute little 'Out to Lunch' sign on the door and come over at noon. We need to discuss the reception."

"The caterer tattled, right?"

"Mr. Pierre was a tiny bit confused about where to set up the steam table for the hot canapés, Claire." The tacit accusation seemed to give her courage. "Noon, or whenever you can get away. It's such a perfect day; I'll have Camille set a table on the patio. Byee . . ."

For all my vices, I am prompt. Shortly before noon, I hung the noticeably uncute, fly-splattered sign as bidden, locked the door, and walked down the railroad tracks.

The Twiller house—more accurately, antebellum mansion—is only a few blocks away, if one takes the obvious shortcut under two bridges and along the gully. It's a pleasant walk. In the spring, wildflowers line the embankment in a lush quilt of colors, and in the summer even the weeds have an unruly charm. Now things were a bit muted, but it was preferable to exhaust fumes and surly joggers who have an irritating possessiveness about the sidewalk.

I scrambled up the path on the embankment and crossed the street. When Azalea's checks started rolling in, the Twillers opted for the staid, dignified side of town. Not that they lost any prestige, of course. The whitewashed brick house was encircled by an ancient iron fence. The sidewalk was original brick. The pillars soared skyward. The ceiling of the porch was painted an appropriate shade of blue. The only thing missing was a quaint statuette of a livery boy holding out his hand. However, it is a truly beautiful house, and I covet it with a pure green envy. The day I write my first lurid romance, I'll put a down payment on a house exactly like it. Caron would fall into the role of Scarlett O'Hara without missing a flutter of her eyelashes.

I rang the bell and waited to be admitted to the temple. Mildred appeared, breathless and dithery. She clutched her toy poodle to her breast in what appeared to be a death grip. Twilliam didn't seem to object; he glared at me with malevolent, black marble eyes, clearly wishing he were free to deal with me in his doggy way.

Mildred tightened her grip, ignoring the rumble that came from Twilliam's throat. "Oh, thank you so much for coming, Claire. I felt a sudden urge to talk to someone, and I thought immediately of you, since you are my dearest friend."

"Mildred, I have about twenty minutes for lunch. I'm also hungry."

"Well, naturally. Let's go to the patio this very second. I know how hard you work all day." She kept up a steady flow of praise for my self-sacrificing devotion, my loyalty, my integrity, and whatever else she assumed I was doing properly those days. Twilliam had a different opinion, but he couldn't wiggle free to make his point with his nasty little teeth.

The patio is shaded by enormous elm trees and surrounded by beds of massive azaleas. In the spring they are, as Caron would solemnly declare, awesome. Mildred does not permit her guests to miss the parallel, and even Douglas seems to find amusement in it. After all, Azalea Twilight does pay the gardener.

The table was set with delicate china and wineglasses. As

we sat down, Camille came out the french doors with a salad bowl and a basket of croissants. I pitched in enthusiastically. Mildred hugged Twilliam and watched me in silence, which finally unsettled me enough to disrupt my momentum. I forced myself to slow down, albeit fractionally.

"So what did Mr. Pierre see as the major problem?" I said, between mouthfuls of shrimp.

"He wasn't sure that you had quite the right attitude," Mildred said in a gently reproachful voice. "He feels that his staff will be endangered if they serve canapés from the middle of Thurber Street. All that traffic, you know."

"Mr. Pierre suggested that we remove all the books so that the guests would be more comfortable. It is a bookstore, Mildred, and not a banquet hall."

"I'll speak to him, Claire." Mildred stared at the vast lawn, as though searching for the words that would pacify Mr. Pierre without incensing me. Wishing her luck, I went back to the shrimp.

Camille refilled our wineglasses, eyed my clean plate, and looked down at Mildred. All of the staff look down at Mildred, without exception. "Will there be anything else, ma'am?" It was not a question; it was a dare.

"No, thank you." Mildred gave me a startled glance. "Unless you'd like coffee, Claire?"

"Black, with sugar," I answered politely. Someone needed to keep the staff busy, and Azalea certainly owed me a favor or two. Camille sniffed rebelliously but silently glided into the house. I wiggled to find a comfortable position in the metal chair, enjoying the afternoon sunlight and sense of well-being that comes with money. Money buys shrimp, peeled by someone else. It buys coffee in porcelain cups, served by someone else. It probably could buy the heart of a carnivorous IRS agent—if he had one.

"Claire, what do you honestly think about sex?"

That jarred me out of the pleasant reverie. "Well," I began cautiously, "I think it may be a bit overrated, but it is necessary for the survival of the species. It has a certain charm."

"But what if it's simply animal lust?"

"Mildred, you are the expert in the field, not me. Surely in one of your books you covered the subject in amazingly complex detail. What's the newest book about, for God's sake? I assume that it's not a catalog for job seekers at the MLA."

"*Professor of Passion?*" She freed Twilliam and watched him scamper away to a flowerbed to do a bit of gratuitous fertilization. "Why, it's about a campus love affair, Claire. The heroine wishes to find fulfillment, to find meaning for her life."

"Via a major in anatomy?"

"I write about love, not sex." The Azalean personality surfaced like a trout that had spotted a dragonfly just above the water. "My heroines all seek a meaningful relationship, a commitment to their hearts. They never engage in premarital sex—unless there's a reason."

"What are we talking about, Mildred? Are you plotting a new book or merely exploring the biological processes that produce babies that grow up to be raven-haired, buxom heroines or arrogant, anatomically blessed heroes?"

Mildred's eyes misted over, as if she had inhaled a dose of London fog. "Love is a complex web."

While I tried to think of a worthy reply, Camille brought my coffee. It was almost white with cream. Camille and I exchanged mute promises of revenge at some later time, and she strolled inside with a smug expression.

I gave the vile coffee all my attention, determined to finish it with all possible haste. In my stomach, the shrimp had commenced a civil war, using various organs as bunkers. Even the croissants had taken sides. I was afraid that the conversation was moving toward an awkward subject—her marriage. The Twillers have a superficially perfect relationship, but Douglas has quite a few other perfect relationships in the wings. Also in his office, in motels, and in the park under the bushes, for all I knew. I presumed that the gossip had finally arrived home.

"Douglas has been wonderful," Mildred said musingly.

I goggled at her. "He has?"

"He thinks I've been working much too hard lately, and that I'm feeling the strain. He suggested that I take a little vacation after the reception, so that I'll be fresh for the lecture tour. He thought Twilliam and I might enjoy Florida. Sunshine and sand. Oranges."

"For a lecture tour?" My mind failed me.

"For the book, Claire. My agent has lined up talk shows across the country, as well as autograph parties, receptions, and speaking engagements. You do remember that I toured for seven weeks when my last book hit the paperback bestseller list?" Mildred asked, implying delicately that I was at best a reclusive idiot.

"Oh, I see." I didn't. "Then the vacation is designed to take your mind off the dilemma of rutting rabbits? Then you'll be refreshed enough to lecture on meaningful fornication?"

Mildred very carefully refolded her linen napkin and placed it next to her plate. "I am seriously toying with the idea of retiring from the literary world. I cannot withstand the constant demands of being a celebrity."

"Quit writing Azalea books? I thought you adored writing, Mildred. What does Douglas think?"

"He's very supportive. He's told me numerous times that my needs come first, that if I am distressed by the necessity of dealing with the publicity, I must cease making personal sacrifices in order to please my fans. They have been more than loyal, but they will find a new author who stirs their souls as much as I have."

"I suppose so," I murmured. It certainly sounded like a direct quote. I swallowed a wild urge to glance at my watch, shriek in surprise at the lateness of the hour, and exit briskly before I heard anything else. Instead, I said, "Have you mentioned this to your agent?"

"Only to the two people I love the most: you and Douglas. My publishers will have to broach the tragic news to my readers in a cautious fashion, so that they will not march on the office in heartbroken protest."

"While we're on the subject of protests, I ought to warn you that the FWO is plotting some sort of mischief in honor of the reception, Mildred. Maggie Holland was sputtering nonsense about a demonstration in front of the Book Depot."

"Poor Maggie. I suspect she's very frustrated." Mildred sighed.

"I suspect she's deranged and capable of causing a major disruption. The sisterhood does not approve of romance fiction. The publicity won't bother me, but I thought you should be prepared for a bit of unpleasantness."

"Women like that are unable to feel fulfilled and, for some reason, have a compulsion to take out their resentments on the rest of us. I shall have Douglas speak to her."

"Maggie cannot be diverted by an avuncular warning from Douglas. She and her cohort have been closeted in her apartment for the last few weeks, painting signs and rehearsing slogans to be screamed at appropriate moments. I just hope you won't have your feelings hurt."

"I'll try to be sympathetic," Mildred murmured. "After all, if nothing else, it will provide a bit of free publicity. Do you suppose the newspaper will cover the demonstration?"

I stared at her. The woman was not crushed by the idea of being labeled a writer of sexist garbage. Book sales and free publicity would give her strength to withstand the insults. Personally, I rather agreed with Maggie and the FWO. I could see that we would all have a charming time at the reception.

I escaped without hearing further of Mildred's career crisis. I promised her that I would negotiate graciously with Mr. Pierre and went out the gate at the side of the house. As I walked down the railroad tracks, however, I pondered the announcement. Hardly earth-shattering from my perspective, but I wondered if Douglas Twiller was truly so willing to abandon such an incredibly lucrative source of income. Or allow Mildred to cease the extended lecture tours that kept her out of town for several months at a time. Conveniently.

Mildred ought to know, I concluded as I went into the store. I did not leave the 'Out to Lunch' sign on the door, as tempting as it was. When Mr. Pierre's secretary called to arrange an appointment, I did not snarl at the innocent pawn, although I had a few comments reserved for the man when he showed up to talk steam tables. I took the ledgers out to the front counter, perched on a stool behind the cash register, and dove into the smudgy numbers.

Students wandered in and out, along with a few real

people. Real people buy paperbacks; students are the only ones forced to pay over twenty dollars for a book they will use for not more than four months. Farber students do not complain, however; they grasp the dollar value of an education, and none of them would be pleased by a paperback version. I made change absently, pointed out the neatly lettered signs above the various sections, and occasionally forayed into the aisles to help the dimmest find textbooks.

Business as usual, or so I presumed. In the middle of the afternoon, the door flew open. Caron and her dearest friend, Inez Brandon, skittered into the store and took possession of the area in front of the counter. They reminded me of gawky, breathless colts.

Caron has my coppery hair and dark green eyes, but her freckles were done by a heavier hand. Her body has taken on an adult dimension that alarms both of us. Her expression, on the other hand, is generally that of a thwarted four-year-old. Eyebrows horizontal, lower lip extended, nostrils flaring like a trotter—my daughter does lack charm.

Inez is quite the opposite, which is probably why the two of them are inseparable—and insufferable. Inez has limp brown hair, limp brown eyes distorted by thick glasses, and a limp, thin body that has not yet stirred in response to pubescent hormones. Her freckles are dim, half-hearted smears. Makeup fades on her face. In contrast to Caron's sulks, Inez cowers. It is effective; I find myself apologizing or being as jolly as a department store Santa Claus on commission.

"What's up?" I asked them.

Caron's nostrils quivered. "Rhonda Maguire told everyone in the girls' room that Inez was a lesbian. I naturally refuted the statement, but then everyone gave me funny looks the rest of the day."

"Oh." I gulped back a sob. "In what way did you refute Rhonda Maguire's statements?"

"I told her that she was a jealous bitch," Caron said. She shoved Inez into center stage. "I think Inez should prove that she is not a lesbian, don't you, Mother?"

Inez's chin wobbled. "I haven't met the right man."

"It doesn't matter when your reputation is at stake," Caron stated mercilessly. Both of them looked at me.

"Are all those words a legitimate part of your vocabulary?" I asked in a stern, maternal voice. Inwardly I was appalled, but not especially shocked. In my innocence I had encouraged Caron to learn to read. She had moved beyond the Bobbsey twins, unless the little scamps had finally grown up after all those decades of perennial childhood.

"In *The Web of Secret Desire,* the heroine risks everything to prove that she has the passions of a woman. She doesn't worry one whit about the 'right man,'" Caron said. She shot Inez one of her beadier stares.

Inez cowered. "In *Love's Sweet Poetry,* the heroine refuses to compromise herself in order to refute the gossip. She says that a pure heart cannot be soiled by innuendoes and disparaging remarks."

We were somewhere between Peyton Place and the butterfly farm, I cautioned myself. Before I could produce the correct balance of common sense tempered with sympathy, they increased the volume of the argument and stormed out the door. I wondered what the pedestrians along the sidewalk would make of the conversation. I wondered where I had failed. I wondered if I ought to call Inez's mother so that the girl could be locked away in a convent.

I finally ran out of wonderings and went back to business.

At seven o'clock, I locked the store and strolled up the hill. Britton had mentioned a cocktail party the next evening. I wanted to wash my hair, paint my toenails a scandalous scarlet, and finish a biography. Caron was supposedly fixing dinner or at least heating two of the entrées so thoughtfully prepared by others and displayed in the frozen-food case at the supermarket, for exorbitant prices.

A figure stepped out of the shrubs. Farberville lacks the criminal element of the larger cities. Here we run to burglaries, drunken driving, and an occasional brawl in front of a bar, all of which are considered acceptable behavior by the locals. We do not yet have muggers and rapists. I did not, therefore, scream and scramble to the safety of the nearest house. Instead, I smiled distantly and veered around the figure—which was female, anyway.

The woman sidled with me. "Mrs. Malloy?"

"Yes?" My stomach made a comment about Lean Cuisine, but I accepted the inevitability of choking out a courteous reply.

"Could I speak to you for a moment?" she said. Her face was long and pale, her dark hair pulled back tightly enough to give her eyes a peculiar Oriental tilt. Her thin body was disguised by an oversize bulky sweater and antique denim jeans. There was a pinched look about her, as if she were being squeezed by support hose. The composite was unmissable; I pegged her as a graduate student.

"You may speak to me for a moment," I conceded wearily. "But why don't you come to my apartment for a cup of coffee? I live in the upper half of the corner house. I'm also tired and hungry."

"I couldn't!" she said in a shrill squeak. She began to edge back toward the shadows, her hands flapping like misshapen white moths.

"It's not the Hilton, but it's not haunted, either. If you have acrophobia, I'll close the curtains and you can stand in the middle of the room." I tried not to sound as impatient as I felt, but I didn't have a great deal of success.

"I've been in your house, Mrs. Malloy. Well, I've been in Maggie's apartment. If she saw me going upstairs, she'd be furious. Please, can't we talk here? It's terribly important."

"We can talk for approximately sixty seconds." My mother trained me to be accommodating, as long as it didn't hurt my reputation or cost any money.

"My name is Sheila Belinski," she said in a soft, urgent voice. "I'm a grad assistant in the fine arts department, and I'm also a member of the FWO. I thought you ought to know that we're planning to disrupt the reception at the Book Depot this Sunday."

"Thank you, Sheila, but it's not a secret. Maggie has kept me informed of all the details, including the ugly chants, ugly signs, and ugly demeanor of the demonstrators. I do appreciate your concern. If that's all . . . ?" I began to inch around her.

She grabbed my arm, terribly earnest. "But I'm afraid Maggie may become violent, Mrs. Malloy. I don't want anyone to get hurt, simply to make a political statement about sexism in literature."

"Violent?" I laughed merrily as I disengaged my arm. "No one could possibly get violent over an Azalea Twilight book. Outraged, possibly; offended, probably. Violent, never."

"You don't know Maggie."

"I do know Maggie, Sheila. Despite all her political fervor, she is quite devoted to her position on the Farber faculty. Douglas Twiller is destined to become the head of the English department, probably by the end of the spring semester. Maggie is an instructor, which means she has no tenure, and she is intelligent enough not to throw tomatoes at his wife."

"Tomatoes?" The woman snorted disdainfully, as if I'd described a sandbox squabble among the nursery school set—who cannot afford fresh produce, realistically speaking. "Maggie is very upset about this book. She won't throw tomatoes."

"She can throw railroad ties, for all I care. Thanks for trying to warn me, Sheila. At the moment, my biggest worry is that I'll collapse on the sidewalk in front of the Kappa Omega house and be swarmed by hysterical coeds bearing herb tea. Good night," I added optimistically as I started walking.

"I warned you." A cold, cold voice.

"Indeed you did," I said over my shoulder. I did pause in front of Maggie's door on the off chance I might hear the clank of howitzers or the clink of Molotov cocktails. I heard nothing, and since the lights were off, it did not strike me as unreasonable. I continued upstairs, smiling to myself.

Caron and Inez were slumped on the sofa, surrounded by a lumpy terrain of paperback books. All the covers had dewy-eyed women gazing lustily into stony-eyed men's faces; both of the characters seemed unaware that most of their clothing had been ripped away by an unseen hand. Or didn't care.

Inez gave me a wan nod, then waved a book under Caron's kinetic nostrils. "In *Ripples of Rainbow Rapture*, the heroine hides in the basement for eleven months with the hero but refuses to permit more than a mild erotic stimulation. She won't make love to him until he finds a priest to marry them. There's no way she could have known that the priest was really a house painter, so it's not her fault."

Caron thumbed madly through a dog-eared book. With a gurgle of satisfaction, she found the desired passage. "Well, in *Tempestuous, Tortured Autumn,* she sleeps with the guy to protect her dead uncle's reputation, Inez. She's willing to make the sacrifice so that no one will find out he's in the Greek underground. That is the point, isn't it? Listen to this. 'Angelica slowly unbuttoned her beige satin blouse as—' "

I shut the door loudly. "It is time for dinner and homework, girls. Inez's parents are undoubtedly frantic to have her join them at the family dinner table for genteel conversation. You, Caron, may begin your homework while I heat something."

"Mother." Caron's eyebrows formed a single line. Her lower lip could have served as a bookshelf, and her chin a hook for a litter bag. She was not reiterating the obvious familial relationship.

I held up my hand to staunch the flood of indignation. "Good night, Inez. Please allow a few minutes before you telephone. I'd appreciate a brief period of tranquillity."

Inez cowered away. Caron arose with dignity and stalked off to her room, muttering her intention to write a letter to *Family Circle* about my lack of basic parental skills.

"Why don't you read something civilized, like *Moby Dick?*" I called through the door.

Caron opened the door and stuck her head out. "I did, years ago. There's a reason why the book wasn't written about a minnow, Mother. After all, the whale wasn't named Moby George. It's a phallic symbol—a variation on the same old thing, just disguised with a lot of boring stuff about old ships."

"What do you know about phallic symbols?"

Caron gave me a lofty smile. "I read Freud when I was ten."

"And where did you get the book?"

"From you, Mother."

I went into the kitchen to read the fine print on the back of the Lean Cuisine box, praying that there would be no symbolism hidden among the nutritional percentages.

THREE

The date of the reception crept relentlessly closer, until it could no longer be assigned to the vague realm of *sometime* or even *next week*. I resigned myself to the inevitability of the event, and even undertook the distasteful chore of negotiating with the caterer. After a lengthy discussion about personal goals, Mr. Pierre and I arrived at a tentative peace.

By Sunday afternoon, several tables covered with hot and cold canapés were squeezed among the book racks. A champagne fountain gurgled from the counter where the cash register normally sat. The dreaded steam table was not to be seen.

Mildred Twiller, a.k.a. Azalea, had arrived several hours earlier to supervise the arrangements with the ubiquitous Mr. Pierre. She was wearing a silky party dress that included all the hues of the rainbow and innumerable gradations. Silk scarves swung from her neck, flowed over her shoulders, and cascaded down her matronly bosom. A harem girl who had splurged her allowance could not have achieved a more colorful effect.

Douglas was there to murmur encouragement and to open the formidable cartons under the table so that Mildred could arrange her offspring to their most salable advantage. He was quite the perfect husband, always at her elbow to nod approvingly or to remove scarf tails from her champagne glass. He looked splendid in a tweedy jacket and turtleneck sweater, the perfect image of a literary adjunct.

While Mr. Pierre and Mildred argued about procedural intricacies, Douglas and I slipped outside. The Book Depot is fronted by a portico, where passengers could unload their carriages and await the arrival of the train without getting their plumage or top hats wet. On rainy days, the pedestrians find similar use for it.

"So," Douglas murmured, his hand on my waist, "Mildred told me that you two had lunch the other day."

I nodded. "Yes, shrimp salad and white wine." That wasn't the answer to his unspoken question, but I had no idea what I was—or wasn't—supposed to know. I slipped away from his touch to watch the traffic congeal at the corner stoplight.

"Your friendship means so much to her, Claire. She thinks you are the model of a perfect woman: strong, self-sufficient, resilient. I must agree with her. After Carlton's untimely demise, you were quite a pillar of strength during the ordeal."

"I had no choice. Caron was old enough to understand what had happened, and I couldn't allow her to see me disintegrate. That's not to say I didn't have a few moments of self-pity during the first few nights."

"It's been eight years, hasn't it?" Douglas edged toward

me, unobtrusively stalking. "I hope you're not still alone in your bed feeling sorry for yourself. It could prove tragic to your physical and mental health, my dear. I would be more than willing to be your foot warmer . . . and lay therapist. It might do you a world of good."

He did this about four times a year, on the average. We both knew the routine, and neither of us took it to heart. I shook my head and gave him a demure smile. "When I am alone in my bed, it is by choice, Douglas. At other times, I am discreet. A virtue you might consider taking up, if I may be blunt."

Douglas laughed in a deep ripple. "Are you referring to that sweet little secretary in the English office? The poor girl was in need of a little extra help with her course work; she simply could not grasp the concept of iambic pentameter. I tutored her whenever I could find a moment of free time."

"How kind of you." I tried for a disinterested expression, edged with disbelief and scorn. A complicated maneuver, that. "The campus is perpetually amazed by your willingness to tutor the undergraduate women, Douglas. It's none of my business; I do worry about your wife, though."

He waggled a finger at me. "It is indeed none of your business, dear Claire. Mildred is very understanding about my concern for my students. Anyway, the girl in question has transferred to another department and I, too, am worried about Mildred. Did she tell you that she is serious about retiring from the romance field?"

"At lunch," I said. "She seemed as if she had already made the decision and said that you were tremendously supportive. I was rather stunned; I assumed that Azalea was in her bloodstream."

Douglas's boyish face sagged, exposing wrinkles I had

never seen before. "Mildred is extremely upset about the current trend in romance literature. Her editors are demanding what amounts to softcore pornography, with lurid detail and extensive foreplay. Mildred feels uncomfortable with such prose. She is embarrassed when she must discuss such things in public or in front of a television camera. The publicity tours drain her. Although I should be saddened by her retirement, I can only sympathize."

"Then you don't mind losing those juicy advances and royalties?" I asked, trying not to sound suspicious.

"Mildred comes first," he said with a sigh. "I couldn't press her to do something unpleasant; she's too vulnerable." His eyes drifted to a distant focal point. "I suppose that's why I married her. Thirty years ago when I first saw her, she was standing in the middle of the sidewalk, stranded by her innate indecision. I've been her buoy ever since, her life jacket in the cold ocean of life."

"The Azalean role has helped her, hasn't it? In the last few years she's finally learned to tread water," I commented. If he preferred aquatic analogies, I was willing to play.

Douglas glanced at me. "Whatever she decides about retirement will be of her own choice. The money is less important than my wife's health and inner well-being. I'll support her."

"I know you will," I said quietly, impressed by the sincerity in his voice. Despite Douglas's propensity for midnight tutorials, he is basically a nice man who is willing to go along with anyone's suggestion—if it's not distasteful. Those sweet young things in his covert escapades are by no means befuddled virgins seduced by a charming, sophisticated professor. They have at least one eye on the grade book and the other might stray to the checkbook.

I don't know why I was delving into all this, since, as Douglas had agreed so readily, it was none of my business. I lectured myself on the indulgence while I searched for an innocuous topic.

"Are you looking forward to the chairmanship of the department?" I asked idly.

Douglas's mouth tightened. "It hasn't been decided yet. There are other candidates for the position."

"Sorry. I thought it was . . . well, assured."

"Ask your dear friend Britton Blake if he feels it is assured. He may tend to offer other scenarios, such as his own name on the ballot alongside my own. The idea is preposterous, but it seems to be out of my hands—for the moment."

"Britton is in contention? He hasn't said a thing about the possibility, but I suppose that doesn't mean anything." I was not doing well on my selection of innocuous topics. Despite my aversion to champagne, I moved toward the door. "Perhaps we ought to join Mildred?"

"How thoughtful of you, my dear." Douglas caught my elbow and pulled me into the store. "Look, Mildred, I've snagged a customer who's desperate to own the first autographed copy of *Professor of Passion*."

I would have described it differently; the word *desperate* would not have been included. I nodded obediently. "Oh, yes. The very first copy."

Giggling, Mildred scribbled her pen name in purple ink across the title page and pushed the book across the table. "How absolutely darling of you, Claire! Cash, check, or major credit card?"

"Cash." I dug out four dollars from my purse, then took a handful of change and the book. I retreated to the bar in front of the paperback mysteries. Once I had a scotch to steady me, I retreated even further and glanced at the cover of my latest purchase.

The Professor of Passion had black hair, gray eyes, and a dimple in his chin. From the arrogant curl of his mouth, I could see he had the hots for the blond temptress in his arms. She had rosy cheeks and sultry hazel eyes. She did not have a blouse, unless one counted the wisp of lace covering her nipples in a slipshod fashion.

The lure of the printed word was irresistible. I scanned the back cover for a hint of the motives driving the couple into such a public display of lust. He was impelled, I discovered, by the messages (and other things) arising from his loins. Stephanie, on the other hand, was haunted by dark secrets from her past, when she had been a fabulously wealthy jetsetter who dined with royalty on yachts and played roulette in Monte Carlo. Now she hoped to escape the notoriety by posing as an innocent college freshman. However, Derek had plans to counter all that nonsense with his demanding lips. Ah, the egotism of youth.

Caron and Inez would undoubtedly find some pertinent social commentary within the pages. Or instructions on the intricacies of premarital relationships, I thought with a shrug. The Bobbsey twins never held hands on the covers of their books. Derek and Stephanie were apt to hold other things—page after page.

Guiltily, I realized that the store was filling up with guests. I waved at Britton, who had been snagged and was now awaiting his opportunity to buy an autographed copy of the book. Most of the people were indeed Farber faculty, friends, or at least acquaintances.

I did spot one of my regular customers, an aged hippie who existed in a science-fiction mist. He must have wandered by and noticed that the store was open, I decided uneasily. At the moment, he was reading the back cover of Azalea's book with a very puzzled expression. His long hair swished across his back like a braided pendulum, and his headband restrained the beads of sweat that popped up on his forehead like tiny, glistening prairie dogs. Perhaps *Professor of Passion* would ease him into the 1980s.

When Britton finally received his treasure, we met at the bar. We both stocked up on the hard stuff, then moved to the back of the store to stand in front of the self-improvement paperbacks.

"Douglas grabbed me at the door," he growled.

"Just drink three dollars and seventy-nine cents worth of their liquor," I advised sweetly. "Then eat an equal amount of those divine crabmeat things. You'll come out ahead."

"I suppose I can use the book for kindling during the cold winter months . . . unless I find a wench to warm my bed. Any ideas about that?"

"I use an electric blanket."

Britton struck his favorite pose and intoned, " 'In bed we laugh, in bed we cry; and born in bed, in bed we die.' Isaac de Benserade, 1612–1691."

"What a charming sentiment, Britton. Shall we move on to another topic, such as end tables or armoires?"

"Whatever you wish, Claire. I understand Azalea has discovered a way to do it in or on every piece of furniture known to mankind. I can personally vouch for the feasibility of tables and chairs, but I have yet to figure out how to—ah, indulge my carnal desires in a hot tub without a great deal of sputtering."

"It's probably covered in his one," I said, tapping Derek's aquiline nose. "By the way, I didn't know that you were being considered for the chairmanship of the English department. Quite a compliment."

Britton's beard bristled and his fingers dug into Stephanie's swanlike neck. "I am the most obvious candidate. Because of the Thurber Farber nonsense, Twiller assumes that he'll sneak in ahead of me. But I've published three more books than he has, and twice as many articles, and—" He stopped himself, took a minute to uncurl his fingers, then shot me a wry grin. "But who's counting?"

"Who, indeed?" I pondered the fact that, although I had bedded the man upon occasion, I had never seen this intensity of emotion before. It was a blow to my ego, among other things. I scolded myself to stop behaving like a certain child I know and said, "Come along, Britton. We must mingle."

"I'd rather mingle with you." He lunged, I sidestepped, and we companionably headed back to the party.

Things seemed to be going smoothly. The store was packed with chattering people, most of whom clutched the obligatory purchase. Several had discovered that it worked well as a canapé tray and later would probably arrive at the same conclusion Britton had about kindling. It would be disloyal for me to add my plans for the book, but it wouldn't squeeze as well as Charmin.

Mildred was clearly delighted with the event. Her voice could be heard above the deafening chatter, elated and thick with Azalean superlatives. And why not? I told myself sternly. It was her moment of glory. Her other books had received national acclaim, but this was the first local reception. The Book Depot's last, in spite of the plentiful scotch and crab thingies.

It took a few minutes to isolate the noise outside from the roar inside. Voices, strident. Anger, vocalized in unison. And not nice at all. I grabbed Britton as a shield and pushed my way to the front door to gaze at the FWO in all its glory.

The FWO turnout was better than average. Maggie had managed to produce about a dozen henchwomen. All of them were dressed in faded denim jeans, bulky jackets, and uncompromising T-shirts that did not meekly advertise anybody's product or resort. Their signs were crude, as were the messages painted in streaky letters. I spotted Sheila at the end of the line, clearly the sergeant-at-arms in charge of stragglers.

Maggie, naturally, was at the head of the line criss-crossing my sidewalk, and her voice was by far the loudest, although somewhat distracted. She clutched a copy of *Professor of Passion* inches away from her Rudolphian nose. Her eyes could have charred the pages. I caught myself wondering if she was prone to motion sickness; it seemed perilous to read in such frenzied transit.

"Sexist smut! Sexist smut!" the feminist soldiers chanted. Cued by an invisible signal, they all switched to "Garbage por-no! Garbage por-no!" A reliable tempo, but less alliteration.

It was quite impressive, I decided as I observed them from the doorway. Britton was snickering into my collar. Most of the guests were beginning to hover behind him; it was only a matter of seconds before Mildred realized that she was no longer the main attraction. Cocktail chatter was rapidly transforming into rude laughter. Although I had mentally prepared myself, I felt a twinge of remorse. It was my bookstore, and the demonstrators were under my roof, so to speak. And they were distracting my guests from their mission, which was to flatter Mildred.

I spun around and shoved Britton and not a few people back into the store. I slammed the door, took a deep breath, and turned around with the warmth of a fundamentalist

Sunday school teacher. "How about that shrimp dip?" I demanded in a challenging voice.

Faculty people spend a lot of time issuing orders, so they are also prone to respond to authority with ovine complacency. They all moved toward the tables, making appreciative noises about the shrimp dip.

I sagged against Britton. "It won't get any worse, will it?" I mumbled into his lapel.

Before he could answer, it got a lot worse. The door flew open and Maggie marched in, waving the notorious book above her head like a picket sign. "Where is Azalea Twilight?" she bellowed, too blinded with rage to see the obvious.

Mildred stood up and beamed. "Would you like me to autograph your copy of *Professor of Passion,* Maggie?"

Maggie turned an interesting shade of mauve. She did a few of the familiar puffs, then produced a noise that would shame the MGM lion. It cut off the last bit of chatter. The stage was hers.

When she was satisfied with the shocked silence, she snarled, "This piece of trash is libelous. To prove my point, we will have an impromptu reading of excerpts from *Professor of Passion,* by Mildred Twiller—or Azalea Twilight!"

She fumbled through the pages much as Caron had done earlier to prove her point with Inez. In the interim, no one breathed. Douglas moved behind the table to put his hands on Mildred's shoulders, perhaps anticipating a collapse. I thought it a valid possibility, since her face was whiter than Stephanie's neck.

Maggie found the passage. "This character is a professor from a small town in Missouri. He has a beard, blue eyes, and a superficially sophisticated demeanor, which means that he drinks French wine," she announced. Then she began to read.

> Blane Brittom held the key to Stephanie's past, and he was willing to use his vile knowledge in order to satisfy the consuming hunger he felt for her slender white body and sculpted breasts. His was a vicious mind; his was a cold heart. He felt safe that Stephanie would never reveal her knowledge of his past. How could she risk her own future by admitting that her younger sister, an innocent child of fifteen, had died during a back-alley abortion, paid for by the very man who stood in the front of the classroom, devouring her with his eyes? She prayed that a similar fate might not befall her, but she realized that his power was mesmerizing, his intentions merciless.

I heard a rather burblous noise behind me, which I suspected came from Britton's throat. It was much like the noises dogs make just before they leap at each other's jugulars. In the name of etiquette, I kept my eyes on Maggie, who was only warming up. She flipped to another dog-eared page.

> Heartbroken and frightened, Stephanie dashed across the windswept campus to seek advice from the only woman who had offered friendship at the campus. Margaret Hollburn had seemed eager for Stephanie's confidences, as though the bonds of sisterhood were more important than any loyalty to her fellow faculty members. Minutes later, Stephanie found herself on the couch in Margaret's shabby apartment, spilling out her heart as if it were an effervescent fountain. Only when her tears began to ease did she discover Margaret's hand creeping up her delicate thigh, intent on that mysterious forest that Stephanie felt belonged only to the man she would one day love.

This time the interesting noise came from our reader, who had to take several deep breaths before she could continue. I risked a quick look at Mildred. She was trembling, her scarves undulating like tiny streams of colored water. Curious, I thought to myself, since she'd written the prose in question; she surely knew that her characters would not be accepted without comment. I looked back at Maggie in time to catch her eyes on me. She dove back into the book.

> Martin Carlow dug his fingers into Stephanie's thick blond hair, forcing her head back so that he could drink in the terror that welled in her eyes. "You will come with me," he said coldly. "We'll drive to the motel to conduct our final examination. When you've managed to please me, I'll take you back to the dorm. But if my wife ever hears of our little adventure, I'll tell Derek the truth about your sister." He raked his eyes down her body as he forced her out the door, ignoring the freezing rain that was already beginning to cover the highway with a treacherous glaze.

I do not make rude noises in my throat. However, I was indeed less than pleased with the excerpt Maggie had chosen to read, and I knew why her eyes had been on me. For a minute I could see nothing but a black wave as the adrenaline rushed through my blood. Like the above-mentioned rain, it turned rapidly to ice. I stared at Mildred.

She met my gaze with two bright, steady eyes, but her chest was heaving in a panicky cadence and the two patches of blusher contrasted with her pallor. Douglas murmured into her ear, perhaps urging her not to have a heart attack at that moment.

The room was still. The people were now mannequins, frozen in position. Mannequins do not, however, audibly salivate at the possibility of a really good public scene. We all carefully avoided one another's faces as the silence stretched into minutes.

Finally, when I was going to scream just to break the

tension, Mildred snuffled. Not the politest sound, but enough to turn on the chatter and send most of the guests to the bar for a refill before the violence started.

Mildred snuffled some more, exchanged a few hurried words with Douglas, and darted toward the back of the store. He watched her for a second, his face taut with concern. I forced myself to unclench my fists before I turned around to see if Britton was slipping bullets into a machine gun.

He was gone. I asked a few spectators if they had seen him leave, but no one had been able to take his eyes off the center ring. Broadway plays cost forty dollars a ticket; the price of admission here was under four dollars, including refreshments. I can't say I blamed anyone. I decided to behave with Emily Post decorum, if not Shirley Temple sweetness, and pushed through the crowd to speak to Douglas.

He was still behind the table, guarded yet anxious. "Claire, I hope you aren't going to make any wild analogies between the characters in the book and real life," he began in a defensive murmur, backing away on the chance I was going to punch him in the wild analogy. He wasn't too far off base.

"I would like to have a discussion with Mildred about her book. Where is she? Reading my diary or pawing through my bank statement?" I demanded with promised E.P. decorum.

"She said she felt a migraine coming on and wanted to leave quietly through the back door." Douglas gave me a blast of the old charm. "I know she had no idea that you—or the others—would react so emotionally to the book. There is a disclaimer in the front of the book that promises that the characters bear no resemblance . . ."

Maggie marched up behind me, and her presence seemed to take the wind out of him. If I believed in auras, I would have admitted there was a definite black haze surrounding her. Thunder and lightning were not far behind. The customary puffing was replaced with an equally disturbing composure.

"Where is Mildred?" she said. Or spat, to be precise.

Douglas ran through the migraine explanation for Maggie's benefit. He then ran his hands through his hair and looked as though he were considering the possibility of running through the door.

"I'm consulting my lawyer immediately," Maggie said. "This is libel of the worst kind, Douglas. Although I never realized that your wife was quite so vindictive, I must say I'm not surprised." She shoved the book at Douglas, who took it meekly and put it behind his back.

"I am!" I said, bearing down on Douglas. "I think all the lawyers in Farberville are going to make a lot of money before this mess is settled. How could she do such a thing, Douglas? All this drivel about how I'm such a valued friend is a bunch of—of drivel!"

I realized I still had the book in my hand. I restrained myself from beating him with it, since he was not the guilty party. But Mildred Twiller *was,* I reminded myself with surprising virulence, and she deserved whatever she got from her petty little trick. Poor Britton and Maggie would have to fight for their careers. Carlton was unavailable to defend himself, but I carried his name. I realized I could have cheerfully murdered Mildred at that time. To my regret, I later discovered that I was not the only one with that idea.

FOUR

Douglas and I were busy staring at each other when my aged hippie tapped me on the shoulder.

"Where do I get this autographed, Claire? I think I'd like to buy it," he said apologetically. It was his normal raspy voice, but his eyes were as opaque as jelly beans. He was the only person present who had missed Maggie's performance, which indicated the extensiveness of his befogged condition. The man was an ambulatory vegetable.

"It's hardly your genre!" I snapped. "Go drink a big glass of champagne and reconsider." I glared until he shuffled away, then swung back to Douglas. "There'd better be a good explanation for this."

"I'm sure there is. Mildred would never do anything to hurt you; she thinks the world of you. Why, just this morning she was telling me how much she admires—"

"Can it, Douglas." I was not in the mood for hearing how divine I was, especially when half of the Farber faculty was poring over the lesser known but nevertheless fascinating details of Carlton's death. I anticipated a titter of amusement at any moment.

Maggie muscled me aside. "I am going home now to call my lawyer. Tell that nasty, foulmouthed bitch that she's going to hear from him in about fifteen minutes." She thudded out, and seconds later I heard her screeching orders to the FWO demonstrators.

"Claire," Douglas began plaintively, "you've got to be—"

"I do not." I didn't.

Douglas was clever enough to read the signals. He coughed and murmured, "Perhaps I ought to call Mildred and make sure she arrived home safely. She was so upset that I'm afraid she might have driven off the railroad overpass."

I took a deep breath. "In that you are a guest in the Book Depot, I will refrain from further comments. You may use my office to call, but then the reception will be over. Understand?"

He gave me a weak smile and disappeared down the aisle to hide in my office. I went back to the bar for a hefty slug of scotch, then plastered a bright look on my face and commenced to mingle with determined gaiety. If I were lucky, only a small percentage of the people would make the connection. Those who did would not be given a free show—from me, anyway. There were plenty of other juicy bits to amuse them. Mildred had not been overly coy with her characters' names. Margaret Hollburn, Blane Brittom, Martin Carlow—for God's sake!

I had misjudged the acumen of those present. After being given at least fifty omniscient smirks, I could no longer stand it. I told Mr. Pierre that it was all his, slipped on a sweater, and went out to see what had happened to the FWO. If there had been an extra sign, I would have snatched it up and let out a few chants myself.

Leaderless, they had dispersed. The street and sidewalk were relatively unpopulated for a Sunday afternoon. A few couples strolled down the hill from the campus, contented with clear sky and shop windows filled with the latest preppie fashions. I snorted to myself and took off down the railroad tracks, my heels leaving crescents in the dirt between the ties.

Eight years ago, when the highway patrolman had knocked on the door, his hat in his hands and his expression tactfully sympathetic, I had heard all the details. The girl in question, although by no means the next Aristotle, had had enough sense to wear a seat belt. Carlton had flown through the windshield; she had at least kept her seat. She was mangled but not terminally so. Her father arranged to keep her existence out of the newspaper and even hushed up her name in the police report. I did not ask. The vision of bloodied chicken feathers had more than dampened my curiosity.

So I had naïvely presumed that no one knew about her presence in the car. I had seen no reason to offer the information to anyone and had donned my mourning clothes like the brave little widow that I was. But now . . .

"How could you do it?" I bawled at the embankment. "Azalea Twilight, I hope you—I hope you—" I sputtered to a halt, embarrassed by my ferocity.

Well, I hoped she was prepared to take the consequences. I was not the only one with a grievance in the community, for that matter. I had never asked Britton questions about his past, preferring not to be bored with lost love, disillusioned irony, or even cherished sexual conquests. I caught myself speculating about the reference in the sordid book and gave myself a pinch. If only the entire population of Farberville would behave with equal self-restraint, we might all survive the scandal. And Peter Pan would appear on my windowsill to search for his shadow.

I realized I was below the Twiller house. The path snaked invitingly up the steep slope; I could see the top of the roofline. Mildred was there, sobbing into a lace handkerchief or reclining on a chaise lounge with a damp cloth over her eyes. How had she found out about Carlton's little passenger? I considered confronting her to demand an explanation. Outraged indignation battled with an ingrained distaste of scenes. Indecision sent me forward and back, as if I were propelled by a piston in my back.

In the midst of all this inner turmoil, I heard Caron's voice above my head. "Mother, what are you doing? Is that some kind of old-fashioned dance?"

She and Inez were hanging over the overpass, Punch and Judy with pimples. I took a second to compose a reasonable explanation, which was not as easy as it sounded, then yelled, "Taking a walk. What are you doing?"

The girls looked at each other. After a hushed conference, Caron giggled and said, "Taking a walk. I thought you were supposed to be having a reception at the Book Depot, Mother."

Inez sighed grandly. "For Azalea Twilight, Mrs. Malloy."

"I know where I am supposed to be," I yelled. What a silly way to have a conversation, I thought. I pointed at the embankment. "Come down and walk back with me. I need some help putting the Book Depot back into its original state. If you'll help, I'll give each of you a paperback."

They scrambled down the path to join me. Caron said,

"Can we have *Professor of Passion* for our Twilight collections? Will Azalea autograph it in person?"

"Oh, yes," Inez added with another sigh, clearly on the edge of a literary orgasm. "Her thirteenth book, you know. It must be divine . . ." More sighs. "I just adored the last one; it was so utterly sensitive. The hero had jade eyes and a mysterious scar on his cheek that he would not explain. His name was Jared."

I gave them a nudge and we started for the store. "I was thinking of something more educational, such as *Pride and Prejudice*. You have no business reading things you don't understand—either of you."

"Mother, I happen to understand everything I read," Caron huffed. "After I read *Professor of Passion,* would you like me to explain any of it to you?"

If we hadn't been ten feet from the store, I might have marched her off to the nearest closet until the speculation faded to a dull murmur. I hadn't considered her potential reaction earlier, when all my ranting was addressed to my personal affront.

Caron and Inez would zero in on *Professor of Passion,* whether they got it from me or from the bookstore in the mall. Caron is not a dolt; she would hardly fail to miss the bit about her father. "Martin Carlow" was not a devious anagram.

Waving Inez ahead, I caught my daughter's arm. "I cannot stop now to talk to you, but I want you to promise me something. Before you read that book, we need to have a long talk. I can't explain here. Will you promise me that?"

Caron toyed with the jutting lip, but finally pulled it in and nodded. A theatrical sigh punctuated the facial display. "I won't read it until we talk," she said, "but I can assure you that I will not be shocked by explicit sex. I know all that stuff already."

She probably did, but she didn't know that her departed father was on the way to a sleazy motel with an undergraduate student when he departed the world in a blizzard of chicken feathers. I wanted to gather her in my arms and make all the maternal noises, as if she were a toddler again, but I knew that the gesture would only offend her. I settled for a sober look and we caught up with Inez.

The Book Depot had nearly emptied in my absence. The hippie was sitting on the floor in front of the champagne fountain, humming tunelessly as he read *Professor of Passion*. I hauled him up and sent him out the door, the book clutched to his chest as if it were a Dune novel. His pockets bulged with canapés, but I overlooked his transgressions and wished him a lovely dinner.

The last few guests made polite farewells and left to read the book aloud over martinis. The Farberville telephone system would be taxed that evening, I suspected as I watched Mr. Pierre's staff scurry about with crumpled cups and napkins. Damn Azalea Twilight, I muttered to myself. I showed the girls what to do, then hunted up Mr. Pierre himself to finalize the cleaning detail.

Mr. Pierre seemed a bit unraveled. "Where are Mr. and Mrs. Twiller, Mrs. Malloy? We have not as yet"—discreet cough—"settled the account. I must pay my staff immediately."

I resisted the urge to tweak his goatee, which looked as if it were made of horse hairs and attached with spirit gum. "Mrs. Twiller is at her home. I have no idea where you might find Mr. Twiller, and I don't believe that I care. Give your staff the remaining crab bites so that they will survive long enough to get their checks in the morning."

Mr. Pierre gave me a decidedly un-Gaulish glare. "Listen, lady, I have bills—just the same as everybody else. Crabmeat isn't dogfood, and I'm not leaving until—"

"There you are!" Douglas boomed, coming down the aisle from the office. He took Mr. Pierre aside, and they haggled over a sheaf of bills until both were satisfied. I caught Caron and Inez eavesdropping and sent them to the office for a broom.

When the last silver-plated tray had been wrapped in tissue paper, Mr. Pierre and his minions disappeared toward the vans parked beside the store. Douglas came over to pat my shoulder. "I spoke to Mildred, Claire. She's appalled that you thought she would ever cast aspersions on Carlton's reputation. Carlton was one of her dearest friends, and she—"

"If I hear one more word about 'dearest friends,' I am going to forget my resolution to behave in a civilized fashion and rip your beard off your chin," I swore in an undertone, smiling for Caron and Inez's benefit. No spirit gum there.

"You may have a point," Douglas acknowledged graciously, as if I were an unruly but promising freshman. "But I know Mildred would like to have the opportunity to explain, so will you please come by the house for a drink later this afternoon?"

"No."

The professorial pose evaporated. Douglas glanced over his shoulder to see if the girls were occupied, and then said, "There is an explanation, Claire. I implore you to give Mildred a chance. She is totally distraught. I don't know what she might do if you don't listen to her."

"All right," I said, unable to resist the same old sympathy for Mildred that had instigated the whole disaster.

"I'll listen, but not over a martini. I don't feel quite that civilized."

"Claire, my darling, I've always known there was a heart of gold under that cold demeanor. We'll see you about five." Douglas hurried out the door before I could react to the cold-demeanor comment.

Caron and Inez had dragged all the paperback racks into place and were busy making their selections. I heard Inez pleading for *Professor of Passion,* but Caron came up with some firm comment that squelched the pleas. They did not, however, choose a children's classic. Not a day for miracles, clearly.

I was extolling the virtues of Joseph Conrad when the telephone rang. As I went to the office, I wondered if it might be Britton. I was stunned to hear a vaguely familiar voice. Sheila Belinski, the FWO sergeant-at-arms, was no longer in contol of anybody, including herself.

"Oh, Mrs. Malloy! You've got to come here right away! The most dreadful thing has happened, and I didn't know what to do, so I thought I ought to call you to see if you could—"

"Hold on, Sheila. I have no idea what you're babbling about, but I'm not at all sure that I want to know." I looked down at the copy of Azalea's book lying on my desk. "Is it about Maggie?"

"Noooooo . . ." The sound evoked images of a coyote silhouetted on a distant mountain peak.

"Well, I don't think I know you well enough to offer advice about your personal affairs," I said tartly. I had enough of my own personal affairs to last for months.

"It's about Mrs. Twiller . . ." she continued. A hesitation, followed by a low, rumbling moan.

"Are you in the book, too?"

"Noooooo . . . Mrs. Twiller is dead! I just found her, and I don't know what to doooooo . . ."

That did get my attention. I gaped at the cover of the damned book, searching for a hint of explanation. Derek and Stephanie had none to offer. "Mrs. Twiller dead, Sheila? Are you sure? I think you'd better call an ambulance immediately, in case you're mistaken."

"I'm not mistaken. She's dead, Mrs. Malloy! Her face is all blue and her eyes are open and bulgy. Her tongue is—oooooh, awful! I can't tell you how awful it—" Sheila broke off in a string of arrhythmic hiccups that gradually faded to sobs.

Bewildered, I waited until I thought she could hear me. "I believe you, Sheila. You call an ambulance, anyway, and sit tight. I'll be there in a minute or two." My brain finally began to operate. "Are you alone? Where is Camille? Where is Mr. Twiller, for that matter? He left here a few minutes ago; he should be home by now."

"I don't know, Mrs. Malloy. There's just me and Mrs. Twiller. The little dog is going to bite me if I don't close it up in a bedroom." She stopped to wait out another string of hiccups. "Thanks, Mrs. Malloy. I don't know what to do—nothing like this has ever happened to me before. I'll wait for you."

The receiver buzzed in my ear. I managed to hang it up, then sat down on my desk. Mildred Twiller wasn't really dead, I tried to tell myself coolly; she was—she was just blue because of her migraine. That was why her eyes were bulgy and her tongue was—whatever it was. Okay, she was dead. That seemed unavoidable. A heart attack? A sudden stroke on the chaise?

Not the case, I decided reluctantly. Corpses did not display distasteful tongues, unless they had not enjoyed a peaceful demise. Carlton's tongue had not been found, but it certainly wouldn't have looked any better. In fact—

I stopped myself inches away from hysteria. Poor little Sheila was doing better than I, and she was babysitting for a dead body with a tongue. I yanked myself to my feet, took a very deep breath, and attempted to smile as I left the office, mentally testing various lies to see if the girls might buy any of them.

The girls were gone. I made it to the door, then stopped and went back to the office to do what had to be done. I picked up the receiver and dialed the emergency number of the police to report the death. The tongue had forced my hand.

Somehow I drove to the Twiller house. A police car pulled in behind me, and two uniformed officers came after me with grim expressions.

"Are you Claire Malloy?" one demanded. He looked as if he were about seventeen years old. Most of them did these days; they must be recruited out of kindergarten. He also looked as if he were anticipating some butterfly-brained lady to attack him with a parasol.

"I am Claire Malloy," I replied with dignity.

"Then why don't you tell us about the body inside the house, ma'am? My partner and I are curious." He was oozingly patronizing, and displayed a noticeable dose of amused incredulity.

"I know nothing about it."

"Then why did you call in the report?" he countered with a gotcha smirk.

The ambulance saved me from a metaphysical discussion of civic responsibility. The ambulance attendants, lugging a gurney and a first-aid box, shoved us aside to hurry up the walk. I shot the policeman a superior look and followed them.

Everybody pushed through the front door and stomped around the foyer in a bovine ballet. I had no idea where to find Mildred's body; I shrugged in response to the terse questions coming from all four sides of me. My credibility hovered at zero when Sheila stepped into the doorway from the living room.

"The patio," she breathed. She took another step forward, clasped her inconsequential bosom, and crumpled onto the floor at my feet.

I tapped the policeman on the arm and pointed down. "Ask her about the body," I suggested as I trailed the ambulance attendants to the patio. A figure lay on one of the metal chairs, a full-size rag doll with floppy limbs and a rubbery neck.

Sheila was right. Mildred was dead, and her facial features were no less gruesome than promised. I took a quick look, clamped my eyes closed, and blundered back into the living room to sit down on the sofa. I was not yet ready to open my eyes when the policeman cleared his throat.

"Would you like a glass of water, ma'am?"

"No, thank you. Is Sheila—the young woman in the foyer—all right? I have a lot more sympathy than I did a few minutes ago," I said, guilty about my earlier conduct. If I had been in Sheila's situation, I'd be on the floor until December.

"My partner is seeing to her, ma'am. But I'm going to need a lot of information about what's happened. Perhaps you could tell me who the woman was or whom we need to notify?" He was trained to be polite in such situations, but I sensed we would never be friends.

I told him Mildred's name. I explained that Douglas had left me a few minutes earlier and had presumably been on his way home. The policeman wrote it all down, then excused himself to call in his report from his patrol car.

I stayed on the sofa and tried to assimilate the scene on the patio. Mildred's body sprawled on the very chair I had sat in when we had lunch. She would never again nibble a croissant or bury her face in Twilliam's fuzz. Poor Mildred Twiller had muddled through life with the fury of a petunia. But she had been a friend—and now she was dead. I almost felt bad enough to recant all the nasty thoughts I'd been harboring for the last two hours.

Poor Douglas, I thought, would be stricken. He loved his wife in his own way; not with the conventional gesture of fidelity, perhaps, but I had seen the emotions on his face when he talked about her. Where was he?

The ambulance attendants wandered into the living room, their hands in their pockets. One of them glanced around for an ashtray, then sighed and went to lean against the wall. The other stared at me, possibly hoping for another victim to pass the time.

"Why aren't you doing something?" I demanded.

"Can't move the body until the CID and the coroner get here. Scene of the crime and all that. There isn't anything we can do to help her now. She's deader than a roast turkey on Thanksgiving."

The second one picked up a porcelain candy dish to read the underside. "Is this an ashtray?"

I explained that it wasn't but advised him to use it anyway. Mildred certainly wouldn't care. We sat in silence until the policeman came back to the room.

"You'll have to wait here until the CID arrives, Mrs. Malloy. They'll want to talk to you and to the young lady," he announced. His expression implied that I was getting that which I richly deserved. Arrested, sentenced, imprisoned, and ultimately hanged; I could read the rosy scenario in his eyes.

The ambulance attendants went outside to wait. The policeman and I gauged each other for a lengthy minute. I was seeing a pompous, authoritative teenager; he was seeing, no doubt, a cold-blooded killer. I escaped to the kitchen to get a drink of water. When I returned, I suspected that my actions had been noted in his spiral notebook: *Killer obsessively thirsty after crime.*

It took the homicide squad more than ten minutes to arrive. Social relations had not improved when two plainclothesmen at last came into the foyer. My blue friend joined them, and after a muted discussion, they all came into the living room to look at me.

I looked right back. The first one had curly black hair, a beakish nose, and guileless brown eyes. He wore a well-cut three-piece suit and a discreet tie, as though he had dashed away from his executive suite to tidy up the situation. He lacked a briefcase, but the image was otherwise perfect. My idea of a Farberville cop included a polyester jacket, an undulating midriff, and a perpetual sneer; this contradiction rather surprised me.

The second man was paler, with a blond crewcut and a bulldog jaw. He was younger, with the eagerness of a high-school hurdler. He waited for the other man to speak. Which he did, once he had finished studying me.

"You're Mrs. Claire Malloy? I'm Lieutenant Peter Rosen of the Farberville CID. We seem to have a problem here, if the reports are accurate. A body." A New York accent, but a pleasant one.

"So it seems, Lieutenant," I said.

He gave me a polite nod and went out the french doors to the patio. Minutes later, a man with a medical bag went through the living room to join them. Uniformed men passed back and forth like windup toy soldiers, their faces professionally masked. No one noticed me for another half-hour. I strained to hear the mumbles from the patio but could make out only a few names—including mine, Mildred's, and Sheila's.

In the interim, Sheila staggered into the living room and flopped across a chair. Her face was white; her long, dark hair fell across her eyes like stray crayon marks. She gave me a numb glance, then sank into the upholstery to study the chintz rosebuds.

"Sheila?" I whispered, not wanting to set off a second display of hysteria. "Are you feeling better? Can I get something for you?"

Shuddering, she shook her head and burrowed deeper. I considered the wisdom of persevering with another question or two, but the reappearance of the lieutenant settled the issue.

"You're the one who called the emergency number of the department?" he asked me.

"Yes, I did. From what I could gather, Mildred had died rather abruptly, and I suppose I've read too many mysteries." I tried to laugh. "I didn't call Scotland Yard, though. Too expensive."

"There are indeed a few points to be cleared up, Mrs. Malloy. The attendants are going to bring the body through this room in a minute, so I thought we might all step into the den." He waited until Sheila and I stumbled to our feet, and then escorted us to the cozy, paneled room on the opposite side of the foyer.

"Now, let me see," he murmured as he closed the door

and turned to smile at Sheila. "I spoke earlier with Mrs. Malloy, but I don't believe you were able to come downstairs at that time. You're . . . ah, Miss Belinski?"

Sheila muttered her full name and, with mild prompting, her dorm address and telephone number. The detective ascertained that she had dropped by to look for a friend, discovered the body, and called me. After mentioning that he would come by her dorm within the hour, he sent her away to recuperate.

Feeling like a first-grader, I raised my hand. "I need to see where my daughter is, Lieutenant. But I will be home if you need me, so why don't I run along, too?"

"I'm afraid I'll need you for a few more minutes," he said smoothly, implying that his happiness depended on my continued presence. "But I certainly won't object if you'd like to call your daughter and let her know that you've been—well, shall we say, tied up?"

He warranted a good deal more flippancy than I could produce at that moment. I went to the telephone and called the apartment. After ten rings, I hung up and tried Maggie's number to ask her to leave a note on the door. Perhaps she was still closeted with her lawyer, I decided glumly. At any rate no one answered.

I hung up the receiver and said, "I'll try again in a little while, Lieutenant. However, I don't see how I can be of any help. I told the officer that Douglas Twiller was, as far as I know, on his way home when I last saw him. He's the one to explain the reasons for poor Mildred's suicide."

"Suicide, Mrs. Malloy? In twenty years I've never seen anyone commit suicide by strangling himself. Pills, guns, slashed wrists, leaps from bridges—yes. Popular choices. But never by strangling oneself with a silk scarf, neatly knotted in the back." The man flashed two rows of even, white teeth at me. A model in a toothpaste commercial would have been shamed.

"She was strangled?" I gasped, no doubt sounding strangled.

"Very thoroughly, Mrs. Malloy." Another of those damned sweet smiles, as if he and I shared a secret. "Now, I am a bit curious about one little thing. In the majority of our cases, the citizen who discovers a dead body chooses to call us. Why did the young lady call you to report the homicide?"

A fascinating question. I gulped under his bright-eyed scrutiny, and managed to murmur, "She was terribly distraught, and I suppose she happened to remember that Mildred and I are—were friendly. I didn't stop to ask questions; it did not seem to be the moment for such irrelevancies."

"And now that you've had a chance to think?"

I shrugged. "Your guess is as good as mine, Lieutenant Rosen." Since mine was nonexistent, I amended to myself as I concentrated on producing a judiciously mystified expression.

FIVE

I described the reception, with an emphasis on the menu rather than the unpleasantness. Lieutenant Rosen seemed unimpressed with my story but was gentlemanly enough not to do more than raise an eyebrow. After I had run out of canapés, I crossed my legs and twitched an impatient foot. "May I leave now?"

"In just a minute, Mrs. Malloy. I understand, from what you've told me, that you were a friend of the deceased. But why did Miss Belinski come to Mrs. Twiller's house to find her friend?"

"I have no idea. Why don't you ask her?" A perfectly sensible answer, I thought. I presumed that the connection was through Maggie, but I had no intention of throwing her to the wolf. Sheila could do the dirty deed.

"And you have no idea where Douglas Twiller might be at this time?"

"None at all."

Lieutenant Rosen gnawed on his lip. "We seem to be missing quite a few people at the moment: the maid, the husband, your daughter, this mysterious friend, the gardener who lives in the carriage house—and a killer. Any suggestions, Mrs. Malloy?"

"I earn a living selling books; I do not receive any renumeration for solving homicides, nor do I operate a missing-persons bureau for the general community. That is more your field, Lieutenant."

"Now, Mrs. Malloy, I agree that you're not an employee of the CID, but citizens are usually willing to help us in a murder investigation. You seem—ah, a shade reticent."

As irritating as it was, it was also true. And I had no idea why I had taken such a truculent posture with the man. I try very hard not to make rash judgments about people, but the man had provoked me into one. Madison Avenue suit, sweet smiles, deferential tone—I wasn't buying any of it. He had the look of a piranha posing as a discolored goldfish. However, it is not prudent to offend a detective who is looking around for a perpetrator.

"I apologize, Lieutenant Rosen," I murmured, lowering my eyes as I sank back on the sofa. "Mildred was a friend, and I'm upset—quite naturally, considering the circumstances. I've never had someone I know get strangled with a silk scarf. Emily Post does not deal with such situations."

The second detective stuck his head in the door. "I've finished with the scene of the crime, Rosen. I'm going to the hospital to see if the pathologist has anything to add about the time of death. Do you know who the victim was?"

"Beyond the obvious?"

"The victim was a well-known romance writer. She wrote a string of sexy novels, right up there with Harold

Robbins and Rosemary Rogers. My wife reads them, then keeps me up half the night for a week trying out these really kinky things. I can't play racquetball for months afterward."

Lieutenant Rosen gave me a wounded look. "Mrs. Malloy mentioned that Mrs. Twiller wrote novels, but she didn't elaborate on the content. Scout around and see if you can find some of the books."

The man nodded and disappeared. The lieutenant and I studied various corners of the ceiling for several minutes. I wondered where Douglas was. I prayed I wouldn't still be in den-detention when he finally returned home to hear the news.

"Mrs. Malloy," Lieutenant Rosen finally said, "I wish you'd be a bit more candid with me. We're not dealing with a case of shoplifting or a failure to yield. Someone—specifically, a friend of yours—has been murdered in a very brutal way."

"Granted. But I don't know why you think I have any information about it. Mildred most likely surprised a burglar or caught the gardener digging up a hybrid to sell on the botanical black market. I certainly didn't kill her, nor did anyone I know. Everybody liked Mildred Twiller; hence, we tolerated Azalea Twilight."

"That is an interesting point. Who was murdered, Mrs. Malloy? A romance writer or a housewife?"

"That is your interesting point, Lieutenant. I need to run by the Book Depot to make sure I locked the back door, then go home and drink a toast to my friend. Call me if I can add anything else," I said firmly. I grabbed my purse and started for the door.

"One other thing," he said as we walked into the foyer. "I'll have to have an official statement about the reception and Miss Belinski's telephone call. I'll let you lock up your store and drink the toast, then I'll come by after I speak with Miss Belinski."

"With a stenographer?"

"The CID branch lacks the resources of Scotland Yard. I'll take it down and have someone type it tomorrow. You will have to run by the station to sign it."

"Wonderful. If I see Douglas Twiller, I'll send him home. In the meantime, happy sleuthing, Lieutenant."

"One last thing, Mrs. Malloy."

"One *last* thing, Lieutenant?" I said, emphasizing the second word with a wry tone.

"Yes, Mrs. Malloy. Please try to remember your exact movements this afternoon, with corroboration if possible. Unless we find the gardener with fresh soil on his hands, we will be wanting to know where everyone was during the hours preceding the crime."

"I was hostessing a reception," I said coldly. "There are approximately seventy-five people who will confirm that. I'll have the guest list for you when you come by."

I stomped across the porch, trying to look terribly indignant, and made it to my car without any obvious tremors. But as I pulled away into the relative safety of the traffic, the lieutenant's offhand request reverberated in my head as though it were an echo chamber.

I had been hostessing the reception—up until I lost my temper and went raging down the railroad tracks to glower at Mildred's roof. Murderously, if I recalled my mood with any accuracy. Not that I had scrambled up the path to follow through on it, I told myself in a virtuous tone. I had merely reminded myself that I was not the only one in town with a grievance. Britton and Maggie were both as furious as I. Maggie had only read a few excerpts from *Professor of*

Passion; she might have missed references to other faculty members.

"Oh, damn!" I said aloud, as I pulled into the weedy patch of gravel I refer to as my parking lot. Mildred might have compromised the entire Farber English faculty. Her murder might have been a departmental effort, à la *Orient Express*. Clearly, the first order of business was to read the silly thing. The second was to decide exactly how much Lieutenant Rosen needed to hear about my actions after the tawdry scene. I do not go willingly to meet lions in the middle of the Colosseum.

The Book Depot was dark and still. I switched on a single light and went back to the office to grab the book I had noticed on my desk. It was not there. I pondered for a moment, trying to remember what had happened to my own personally autographed copy. I had used it for a canapé tray but then had put it down somewhere when I heard the first stirrings of the FWO demonstration.

It was hardly worth stealing—especially when everyone in the room had already been coerced into buying one. Surely no one would want two copies of *Professor of Passion*. None of us had wanted one—until we heard the juicy parts from Maggie. It was now a hot item in Farberville.

I checked the back door and returned to the front of the store. The last few unsold copies of the book were in a carton behind the counter. Poor Azalea Twilight would never again take up her purple pen, I thought sadly. The world of prose would survive; I could only hope the widower would do the same. I stuffed a copy in my purse.

I locked up and drove home. A splatter of rain caught me as I dashed to the porch. Once inside the house, I stopped to stare at Maggie's door. No line of light spilled from underneath it, nor were there any muffled noises beyond it.

I went up the stairs to my own apartment. I was relieved to find a note from Caron taped on the door. It said, amid curlicues and heart-shaped dots, that she and Inez had gone to the Farber library to work on reports for world government. I didn't believe it, but I certainly wasn't in the mood to explain what had happened in the last few hours. They, if no one else, would be devastated by the loss of Azalea Twilight, their favorite author.

I dialed Britton's number, but he wasn't home. For the best, I told myself as I made a pot of coffee and a sandwich, then settled down at the kitchen table to discover Stephanie's dark secrets and Derek's winsome technique.

I came out of the sensuous quagmire an hour later. Stephanie did indeed have some dark secrets, and everybody but Derek seemed to be aware of them. He just kept nibbling her throat and whispering endearments. Stephanie clung firmly to her virtue, despite a boggling array of invitations from the faculty. But I didn't spot any references to the Farber crowd beyond the three already known to me: Britton, Maggie, and Carlton.

Footsteps thudded up the stairs. I went into the living room to admit Lieutenant Rosen. His dark curls were flat, plastered over his head like a wet beret, and his coat was dripping copiously on my rug.

"It's raining," he explained, in case I was incapable of piecing together the clues.

"You *are* a detective!" I took his coat and tossed it over the railing at the top of the landing. "Would you like a cup of coffee?"

"I don't suppose you have any bread crumbs on the floor

that I might sweep up and munch?" he said. "I haven't had a chance to eat dinner."

I thawed a bit at this sign of human frailty and led him into the kitchen. "The roaches carried off the last bread crumb. You'll have to settle for a sandwich, Lieutenant."

He followed me to the kitchen and busied himself with creating a tower of bologna, cheese, lettuce, tomatoes, and pickles. When he seemed satisfied with its caloric content, if not its structural integrity, he took an empty plastic milk carton out of the refrigerator. After an optimistic shake, he replaced it and began to shift jars around the shelves. "I don't suppose you have any beer?"

I have read thousands of mystery novels since the first was slipped between the bars of my crib. Although I prefer the English whodunit variety, I have dipped into jaded private eyes, secret agents, and an occasional police procedural. In not one of them did the investigating officer paw through the suspect's refrigerator or demand a beer.

"How about a glass of wine? Then we'll build a fire and play Scrabble," I said coldly.

"That sort of thing will have to wait until later," he said through a mouthful of sandwich. "This is official business. Can't drink wine on official business. Just beer."

I shrugged. Still chewing, Lieutenant Rosen picked up the copy of Azalea's book and glanced at the cover. When his eyes slid to me, I shrugged again. We both looked at each other for a long time, but there was none of Derek's warmth in his eyes, nor any of Stephanie's smoldering passion in mine. At last I tried one final shrug, laughed lightly, and said, "For old times' sake."

"I heard there was a lot of old times' sake in it. Good old Martin Carlow, for one thing. A rather unpleasant reference to Britton Blake, and another to your downstairs neighbor."

"I didn't realize you'd spent the last hour swinging from the proverbial grapevine, Lieutenant Rosen. Perhaps you ought to spend more time looking for fingerprints?"

"Don't show up on silk," he said. He stuffed the last of the sandwich in his mouth. "Damn shame."

"Lieutenant Rosen, if you're finished with dinner, I'd prefer to get this over with so that I can go to bed."

"Does that mean we don't play Scrabble?"

"I'm beginning to be awed by the relentless acumen of the Farberville CID," I said. I went into the living room and sat down on the arm of the sofa. "Are you ready to take my statement?"

"Well, I was going to tell you what Miss Belinski had to say about calling you, but if you're not interested . . ."

The man was a worse tease than Stephanie, I decided. Of course I was interested, but I certainly wasn't going to beg. "All right, tell me," I pleaded.

"Tell me, please," he corrected me. I could almost hear him chuckling triumphantly, which did nothing to endear him.

"All right—tell me, please!" Before I shove you out the window, parachutes not available at this time. Inquire tomorrow, from traction. I smiled, but not at him.

"The young woman says that she called you because she wanted to give you an opportunity to explain. She said she saw you earlier near the Twiller house."

"She did not!"

"She did not—what?"

"She did not call me to give me an opportunity to explain!" I snapped at him. And I had thought my daughter was insufferable! When I had regained a bit of self-control, I managed to repeat the gist of the telephone call, from the first howl to the final click. "So Sheila simply called for advice," I concluded firmly.

"But she did see you near the Twiller house?"

It was getting a bit sticky. I sat down on the sofa and tried to look rueful. "Although it has nothing to do with poor Mildred's death, I was going to tell you that when you took my statement, Lieutenant."

"Then why don't you rehearse it now?"

I told him about my innocent stroll down the railroad tracks to the bridge. The details about my mood struck me as inconsequential, so I omitted those. I concluded with meeting Caron and Inez and taking them back to the Book Depot to help with the restoration.

"So you were gone about thirty minutes?" he asked, making squiggles in a battered notebook.

"And I did not go up the embankment to the house. Write that down in your little book," I said with a show of spirit. Strictly show. "I would imagine it takes a long time to strangle someone."

He peered down his beak at me. "Not really. It doesn't take long to flounce down the railroad tracks to that bridge, either. Certainly not more than five minutes each way. That leaves about fifteen minutes unaccounted for, Mrs. Malloy."

"I was strolling," I countered in a patient voice.

"Miss Belinski described it as a 'flounce,' but perhaps it's a matter of semantics."

"Very possibly. And where was Miss Belinski, anyway? I went out front to see if the demonstration was over, but I didn't see her lurking around to analyze my posture. Did she get her information from a spy satellite? A periscope?"

"She was walking down Arbor Street when she happened to glance at the railroad tracks. She thought you looked dangerously angry, but she assumed you were simply walking it off. Later, she said, she began to wonder about it."

"Later? When she was standing over a dead body? Is that the 'later' we're discussing? Just what was she doing inside the Twiller house?" At this point, my voice might have carried to the Twiller house.

"She admitted that she was looking for a friend of hers, Miss Margaret Holland. It seems that Miss Holland flounced off with the same expression that you had. Miss Belinski said that she went to the house and waited on the porch for someone to answer the door, but became suspicious when all she heard was the dog yapping. The door was ajar." He beamed at me for a minute, then said, "Let's discuss the alleged flounce further, shall we, Mrs. Malloy? I'd like to get a precise picture in my mind of your movements."

I saw no reason to point out that Britton had also flounced into the sunset. It seemed as if Farberville had been rife with flouncers earlier in the afternoon—an unsettling idea. I briskly repeated my version of the stroll, stressing the leisurely manner in which I admired the autumn hues of the foliage along the gully. He listened without comment. A diversion seemed propitious.

"Sheila must have done quite a lot of wondering," I sniffed, making it clear that I had dismissed her statement as trivial mental meanderings.

"Aloud," he agreed cheerfully. "By the way, Douglas Twiller finally showed up. He said he had taken a drive to think about the situation, since he was so upset about everyone's reaction to his wife's newest book."

"Was he—did he handle the news?"

"He looked fairly gray about the gills. One of the

uniformed officers found the doctor's name by the telephone and called him. Twiller's sedated for the night."

"Poor Douglas. He really did love his wife, although he had an odd way of showing it," I said, staring at the floor.

"As in sleeping with half of the campus population?"

"But," I said, "I don't think he meant anything by it. Douglas is an amiable person; if the invitation was couched politely, he wouldn't dream of refusing. I doubt he ever stalked some virginal coed."

"Like our villain Blane Brittom in the book? Of course, he was moving in teeny-bopper circles."

"You have been a busy boy since I left the Twiller house. You timed the distance to the bridge, listened to Sheila's fairy tale—and read a trashy novel. I'm impressed."

He gave me a modest smile. "Jorgeson did some of it."

We both contemplated Jorgeson's activity in silence. At last I took a deep breath and said, "I have not been behaving well at all. I apologize for what I hope will be the last time. Now, may I ask a question?"

"You may ask."

"Why are you so concerned about those of us who were at the reception? Why couldn't Mildred have been attacked by a burglar or one of the druggies?"

"Unless she was a particularly gracious hostess, I don't think she would have offered tea to a burglar—do you? And the coincidences are a bit too thick to be overlooked." He began to tick them off on his fingers. "The woman has written a book that damages at least three reputations; she goes home with a convenient migraine; she ends up strangled on the patio after tea. In such a case, we do tend to have a look at those involved."

I met his eyes. "Do you think I'm involved?"

"Of course. That doesn't mean I think you went to the woman's house to strangle her with a silk scarf, however."

"Thanks," I muttered, with as much grace as I could muster.

"But that doesn't rule out the possibility," he said. "You're a wonderful suspect. You have motive and opportunity. You were spotted near the scene of the crime, apparently with clenched fists and a grim scowl. Mrs. Twiller would have welcomed you into the house, offered you tea, and escorted you to the patio for a chat."

"And asked me to tighten her scarf, no doubt." It sounded pretty good. Mildred would have done exactly what the lieutenant had described. I held up my wrists. "Put on the handcuffs and drag me to the interrogation room. Although I know I'm innocent, I see no reason why you ought to believe me."

"I think we'll wait a few days before we dig out the rubber hoses and cattle prods, Mrs. Malloy. Scrabble is one of my favorite games. And there are a few loose ends to be tidied up."

The steel bars receded a few centimeters. I looked at him and asked, "Such as?"

"We are a bit curious about Douglas Twiller's drive. We haven't been able to locate either Miss Holland or Mr. Blake, and we would like to talk to both of them about their actions."

"Is Sheila Belinski in the clear?"

"She doesn't seem to be involved, beyond the discovery of the body. She has never met the victim, nor is she mentioned in the book."

"But she is a member of the FWO," I pointed out. I told him about the encounter with Sheila several nights ago on the sidewalk, and her sputtered warnings about violence.

But I had to concede that Sheila had not implied that she felt especially strongly about the threat of sexist brainwashing and had only been concerned about Maggie. Lieutenant Rosen seemed mildly interested, at best.

We weren't getting anywhere. The lieutenant wasn't going to tell me anything, and it was possible I knew more than he. I reminded myself that he was trained to deal with recalcitrant witnesses and half-truths. He could figure it out himself.

I stood up. "Well, it's been a lovely evening, but I have to get up early in the morning. If there's nothing else . . . ?"

He advanced like a pin-striped bulldozer. I could see the fine web of wrinkles around his eyes as he grinned, and the tattletale gray hairs mixed among the black curls. "One more thing, Mrs. Malloy, before I leave. I'm very curious about Mrs. Twiller's insinuations in her last book. We've already sent queries to certain people at other colleges, but we need to know if her information is true."

My back hit the wall, in more ways than one. "I'm not available as a spy or a snitch. The people involved are my friends, and I will not gossip about them. You can ask Maggie if she's ever approached a female undergraduate with amorous intent. You can ask Britton if he financed a back-street abortion."

"But they won't tell me."

"What a coincidence—neither will I."

"Won't you?" he murmured, as he went onto the landing to pick up his raincoat. I heard his low chuckles as he went down the stairs. The front door closed with a loud click.

I realized I was trembling. The man was evil, I told myself as I closed my door, went into the kitchen to get *Professor of Passion*, and retreated to my bedroom. I left my clothes on the floor, put on a comfortably shabby chenille robe, and crawled into bed. I turned to the page where I'd left off earlier.

Stephanie was in deep trouble, and her only hope lay in confiding in Derek. But the silly thing was determined to solve her problems without any help from her would-be lover and was floundering from one mess to another. I finally slammed the book shut and tossed it on the floor.

"What a goose," I said, as I gazed at the ceiling. A few niggling parallels came to mind, but I refused to notice them. Poor little Stephanie was a bubblehead, whose age had surpassed her IQ a decade ago. She deserved everything she got—except for the inevitable sugary conclusion.

I, on the other hand, was an intelligent, autonomous woman with a daughter, a store, and a myriad of responsibilities. I didn't have the energy to flounder. But neither was I willing to be convicted of bumping off poor Mildred, or even Azalea. Not if I could help it, anyway.

SIX

The next day I dug a suitably mournful dress out of the back of my closet and walked the few blocks to the Twiller house. I rang the bell, resisting the urge to twist a handkerchief in my hands. Too Azalean, I lectured myself as I assumed a suitably mournful expression. Camille answered the door.

"Yes, Mrs. Malloy?" she said politely. Despite the tone, the challenge simmered just below the surface. Camille was a graduate student in the English department. She was in the wrong field; with a little training, she could have a brilliant career in theater.

"I came by to express my sympathy to Mr. Twiller. Is he up?"

"Yes, he's having coffee in the dining room." Camille held her position, clearly determined to protect the fortress—and the door—on the chance that I was a scout for a marauding Indian war party.

I brushed past her into the foyer, then halted and turned back to study her. "Where were you yesterday afternoon, Camille?" I asked. "You missed all the excitement."

"I have a midterm paper due this week," she said in a sour voice. "Mr. Twiller gave me the afternoon off to go to the library. I didn't get back until about eight o'clock. I heard that you were here . . . with the police."

Touché. I gave her a meaningless nod and went on to the dining room to make the necessary condolence call. Douglas was slouched in a chair, the morning newspaper scattered on the floor. A mass of bacon and eggs had congealed on the plate in front of him. He glanced up at the sound of my footsteps and tried to smile.

"Claire, how nice of you to come by." His hand fluttered in the air, then dropped to his lap. He stared at it through dull eyes.

"Douglas, I'm so sorry about Mildred," I began. "If there's anything I can do, please let me know."

"It's been a nightmare. The police have taken over the house. They've hounded me with questions, but I just don't seem to know anything that might help identify the brutal person who—" His voice, usually so warm and rich, crackled to an abrupt stop. He dabbed his eyes with a napkin and looked away. "Who murdered Mildred," he added in a whisper.

I could imagine Lieutenant Rosen dogging Douglas through the house, the spiral notebook at hand in case Douglas offered an indiscretion or contradiction. The husband is always the first suspect, I tried to remind myself, but Douglas looked incapable of squashing a zucchini.

"I'm sure it has been awful, Douglas," I murmured sympathetically. "But the CID is doing everything it can."

"The policeman seems inordinantly obsessed with my

drive yesterday afternoon. I didn't pay any attention to where I went, Claire. I was just driving—and thinking. Poor Mildred was so stricken by the hostility at the reception. She didn't really have a migraine; she went home to cry."

I took a deep breath. "I'm sure she did not mean to attack any of her friends." Hypocrisy soared to a new height, but Douglas seemed pitifully grateful.

"She really didn't. You must realize that she didn't have a folder filled with dark secrets about her friends. She didn't know that Britton had—well, had an unsavory involvement with a child. She had no idea that Maggie might have perverted sexual preferences, or that Carlton was . . ."

"She certainly was feeling creative, then," I said acidly. "How did she come up with that absurd story about her nasty Martin Carlow taking a coed to a motel? It's hardly something one would fantasize for the fun of it. It was too vicious for that."

"Mildred may have made a mistake by using the names she chose," Douglas admitted. He took a sip of coffee, shuddered, and put the cup back on the saucer. "Camille!"

Camille glided in immediately, undoubtedly having been listening through the kitchen door. "Yes, Mr. Twiller?"

"Mrs. Malloy and I would like fresh coffee. Are there any croissants in the freezer?"

I remembered the luncheon on the patio. "Not for me, thank you. I will have a cup of coffee—black, please."

The corners of Camille's mouth curled slightly as she nodded. After she left, Douglas leaned back to study me. "I suppose we'll have to forgive Mildred's little prank, won't we? She won't have the opportunity to defend herself, or even explain."

"Did she really have an explanation?"

"She said that she did, but I have no idea what it would have been. Perhaps it was a misunderstanding on everyone's part." He seemed content with that, as though the issue were now laid to rest, along with the author. The telephone near the door rang.

"I've had numerous calls from the publishing world already," he explained, with a trace of satisfaction. "The romance industry is quite panicked by the news. Editors, the agent, even hysterical fans . . . the telephone has been jangling since the eleven o'clock news last night. I'll just be a minute."

I politely tuned out the telephone conversation and pondered Douglas's glib assurance that Mildred would have explained everything, had she not been so crudely silenced. How could there have been an explanation? For one thing, nobody knew about Carlton's passenger, except for the brief mention in the police report. The police reports were not open for public perusal—how could Mildred even have guessed that Carlton was not alone?

The second point was that even Azalea Twilight knew the intricacies of libel law; she could never have hoped to avoid a backlash of legal suits and ugliness. That brought me back to Maggie's departing threat. I decided to ease into it.

When Douglas returned to the table, I said, "Has anyone from the department been by yet?"

"Several have telephoned and promised to come by later. The funeral will be Tuesday morning at eleven, by the way. Now I must spend the day sorting through poor Mildred's papers and trying to prepare things for the lawyer."

It sounded like an invitation to leave, but I ignored it. Camille came in with two cups of coffee. Mine was black. I acknowledged the petty triumph with a ghost of a smile. One to two, but at least I was on the scoreboard.

I looked at Douglas over the edge of the cup. "Are Mildred's affairs in order, then? Any novels to be published posthumously?"

Douglas brightened. "One, actually. It's already with the editors and ought to be ready for publication within a month or so. I think I'll retitle it *Bittersweet Farewell*. Mildred would have liked that, don't you think? A final tribute to Azalea Twilight's incredible success."

"Mildred would have adored it," I agreed. "Surely a bestseller."

"Surely." Douglas managed to restrain himself from rubbing his hands together gleefully, but only barely. He finished the last of his coffee, resumed a woeful expression, and said, "I fear I must hearken to my sad duty, Claire, as painful as it may prove to be. Why don't you come by late in the afternoon? A few people will be dropping by to offer their condolences."

This time it was impossible to ignore the invitation to leave. I made a few more sympathetic comments and left. When I reached the curb, I gazed at the top of the path that led to the railroad tracks. On both sides there were brambles dotted with tiny white flowers to disguise the thorns. No scratches on my legs, Lieutenant Peter Rosen, I sniffed to myself as I turned to follow the sidewalk. I doubted that it would help, but one never knew.

By nine-thirty the Book Depot was open and ready for a customer. I immersed myself in invoices for an hour, then met the delivery truck in back to check a shipment of books from the distributor. The driver presented me with a new stack of invoices and rumbled away. It took several hours to unpack the boxes and rearrange shelf space, but I enjoyed the mindless labor.

Afterward I continued with the paperwork, but the third

time I tripped over the box behind the counter, I slammed down my pencil in disgust. Abruptly I was swamped with remorse. The box contained the copies of *Professor of Passion* that Azalea had not sold. Would never autograph. I took the dozen or so copies out and stuck them on the fiction rack. So I refuse to sell romance novels. I could make the gesture for poor Mildred Twiller, a.k.a. Azalea Twilight.

To my chagrin, the books were not swooped up by the customers who straggled by in a steady but thin flow. By noon I was beginning to regret my noble gesture. Derek and Stephanie now seemed to include me in their amorous gazes, as if inviting me to indulge a bit in a ménage à trois. I caught Derek watching me out of the corner of his eye.

"Cut it out, you lecherous goon," I told him tartly. "Why don't you give Stephanie a little more sympathy?"

"The first symptom of schizophrenia is conversing with inanimate objects," Britton commented from the doorway. He came in and brushed his beard against my cheek, then marched across the store to study the foreign-language dictionaries with an intent expression.

I must admit I gaped at his back for several minutes. Finally I pulled myself together and said, "I suppose you heard about poor Mildred?"

"At length this morning," he said. He picked up a Russian-English travel guide and flipped through it, making clucking noises as he shook his head. Over the Russian alphabet or Mildred's demise—I wasn't sure which.

"And who was the bearer of the sad tidings?" I asked when I tired of trying to decipher his back.

"A cop." Britton replaced the book and turned around. "A detective named Rosen, who seemed to feel that I might have gone to the Twiller house yesterday afternoon to scream invectives at poor Mildred. I can't imagine why."

"Lieutenant Rosen heard all the grim details about the contents of the book. He had the very same idea about me."

"And did you?"

"Did I what?" I snapped. Although I nurtured a few doubts about Britton, I did not appreciate the reciprocity.

"Go by the Twiller house to scream invectives at poor Mildred?"

I narrowed my eyes. "Of course not. Why on earth would I do that?"

"Well," Britton sighed, turning back to the dictionaries, "the reference to Carlton was not easy to overlook."

"There was absolutely no truth to it, however, so I had no reason to attack Mildred. Carlton was by himself when the chicken truck rammed him. I wasn't thrilled by her character's name, but that doesn't mean the insinuation had any validity." I forced myself to laugh gaily at the absurdity of such an idea. Wherever Carlton was, I hoped he appreciated the effort.

"And what about the other nasty little suggestions?"

I wished Britton would turn around so that I could see his face, or at least as much as was visible above his beard. His voice was light, but his shoulders were tense. "What about them?" I asked, with equal lightness.

"Do you believe that I paid for a sleazy abortionist to tear up the insides of some little girl?"

Well, we were making some progress. I went around the counter to join him in front of the rack. He refused to meet my eyes. His jaw was squared and hard.

"No, I don't," I said softly. "I have no idea why Azalea Twilight would ever come up with such a patently crazy story. I never believed it for a second; I know you better than that."

The jaw receded, the shoulders eased. Britton put his arm

around my waist and gave me a hug. "Thanks, Claire. I must admit I was unsettled by the parody of my name being used in a trashy novel, but the whole thing was nonsense. Now I have only to convince the rest of the faculty." He sighed at the enormity of the chore. "I suspect I won't be appointed chairman of the department. Twiller would have gotten it anyway. He has the perfect degree of pompousness for the job. I'm too charming."

"Is that your problem?"

"I wish it were," he said. "The problem is actually trying not to be offered a tactful year's leave of absense."

"I cannot believe Mildred really wrote all those horrid things. Douglas swore that there was an explanation, but we never had the chance to hear it. What on earth do you think it could have been?"

"With that woman, anything was possible—including coitus on a trapeze. But let's not worry about it, Claire. Do you still want to go to the gallery opening tonight at the Fine Arts Center? We can go back to my flat afterward to work on erasing the unpleasant memories."

"No, Douglas invited me over for what I suppose will be a martini-soaked wake. Your presence would be in order, I imagine."

Britton tightened his grip on my wrist and began to nuzzle my ear. I freed myself and gave him a sweet smile. "Later—maybe. But you never did tell me where you went yesterday after the impromptu reading of *Professor of Passion*. You rather vanished."

"I made a grand tour of the bars. As a matter of record, I hit every one of them and lingered at more than a few. I was thrown out of the last one well after midnight and blearily wended my way home to pass out on my bathroom floor. 'Not drunk is he who from the floor can arise alone and still drink more; but drunk is he, who prostrate lies, without the power to drink or rise.' Thomas Love Peacock, 1785–1866. There, love of my life, you know the worst about me. Why don't you let me demonstrate the best?"

"You went on a drunk because your name was parodied in a romance novel?" I said incredulously. "Maggie's response made a bit more sense; she went to call her lawyer."

"Did she?" Britton mocked my tone.

"I don't know that she actually did, but she certainly was intending to when she left the Book Depot with steam curling out of her ears. Do you have a reason to believe otherwise?"

Britton gave me a boy scout salute. "Heavens, no. Now, what about tonight after this tasteless faculty version of a wake? Shall I lay in a bottle of burgundy and a piece of brie? We can build a fire in the fireplace and watch the cheese melt."

It brought back a scratchy little memory of a comment from the previous evening. Busying myself with an invoice, I said, "I doubt I'll be in the mood, Britton. Let's save it for another time, shall we?"

He gave me an obligatory leer and left. I dropped the pencil to stare at the empty doorway, thinking about Britton's explanation of his movements the day before. It was not easy to picture him bumping elbows with the local cowboys or even drinking a beer. Britton's taste ran to dusty, obscure bottles of imported wine. It did run to drafts of beer or raucous music. I was surprised that he was even aware of the vast number of bars lining Thurber Street.

The day drifted on. I rather expected to see Lieutenant Rosen, but he did not come to the store. Caron and Inez breezed in toward the middle of the afternoon, more subdued than I had ever seen them. I raised an eyebrow at the black ribbons pinned on their blouses. "New fad?"

"It's for Azalea," Inez explained with a stricken look. "I just cannot accept that she's really . . . gone."

Caron homed in on the *Professor of Passion* on the fiction rack. She picked up a copy and stared at the cover, then spun around to flutter her eyelashes at me. "Why are these here, Mother? I thought you refused to sell them—on principle."

"They were left over from the reception. It seemed like the thing to do," I sighed. Although I had broken the news about poor Mildred to Caron the previous night, we hadn't had the energy to discuss that which needed to be discussed. I could almost see the electrons zipping through Caron's brain as she scanned the back cover of *Professor of Passion*. A bad omen.

Inez sniffled into a tissue. "Can we attend the funeral, Mrs. Malloy? I'd like to pay final tribute to Azalea."

"That is between you and your parents." I spotted Caron's lip inching out and added, "I suppose that I'll permit Caron to go, if she wishes. But it will be a dreary affair, girls. No soliloquies or readings from her work. Organ music, sermons."

"I've been to a funeral," Caron said abruptly. She jammed the book back in the rack and looked at Inez. "Let's go over to the Piggie Pizzeria and see if they have any new video games."

Inez cowered, her expression as bewildered as my own. "I thought we were going to write a eulogy about Azalea for the school newspaper? How she was so thoroughly romantic, so willing to explore the essence of true love . . ."

"Well, we're not. We're going over to the Piggie Pizzeria to see if they have any new video games," Caron said in a tight voice. Then, as if ashamed of her tone, she tried to smile. "I heard some of the kids planning to hang out there this afternoon. It might be fun, Inez."

Inez shot me a look of desperation but meekly followed Caron out the door. I picked up my pencil, then let it drop again. Caron and Inez were not noted for their social skills and had never, to my knowledge, admitted enjoying the company of any of their peers. A strange day, indeed. I made a solemn promise to myself to talk to Caron before the day was over.

An hour later, I closed the store and went home to change for the cocktail wake. As I considered the proper attire, I heard a door slam below. Maggie, I deduced with customary brilliance. I hastily pulled on a wool skirt and beige blouse, ran a comb through my hair, and scurried down the stairs to catch her before she disappeared.

She yanked open the door and scowled. "What do you want?"

"I'm on my way to the Twiller house," I extemporized, perplexed by the show of hostility. "Do you want to walk together?"

Maggie stared at me. "I can't; I'm waiting for someone. Besides, I wouldn't enter that libelous, foulmouthed bitch's house if it guaranteed tenure. Not that anything will guarantcc tenure now."

"Oh." I took a second to think, then said, "Did you talk to a lawyer about suing?"

"Yes. I'm just sorry Mildred Twiller can't be here to suffer." Maggie's eyes began to glitter, and drops of spittle foamed in the corners of her mouth. "I'm going to sue her estate for defamation of character. I'll take every penny of that bitch's royalties for *Professor of Passion!*"

I retreated from the acid rain that splattered across my

face. "Then you did consult your lawyer yesterday afternoon?"

"Are you playing Tuppence Beresford, Claire? Would you prefer me to type up a statement of my whereabouts and slip it under your door?"

I certainly did, but I doubted it would happen. The situation called for humbleness tinged with remorse. "Oh, Maggie, I didn't mean to imply that you had anything to do with poor Mildred's death. The detective has been hounding me for an alibi, too. He acted as if I were his prime suspect, simply because I took a peaceful stroll down the railroad tracks to let off some steam."

I paused in case she wanted to offer her alibi in response to mine. After a moment of glacial silence, I added, "Britton said he was questioned this morning. We're all suspects, Maggie."

She mellowed a bit at my confession or at the idea of others suffering along with her. "That Rosen man was here at eight o'clock this morning, all smiles and apologies for disturbing me. He took my statement without saying much and let me leave for my first class. He seemed satisfied."

"What did you tell him?"

"I told him where I was. Out."

"Did he say anything about further questions?"

"No, I told him that I had no idea about the murder. I wasn't anywhere near the Twiller house and couldn't have seen anything. I didn't threaten to murder Mildred; I threatened to sue her. The detective appreciated the fine difference."

"So you were at your lawyer's office at the time in question?" I crossed my toes, hoping the confidence would not halt until I heard the whole story. Or the lawyer's name.

"Well, I wasn't flouncing down the railroad tracks," Maggie snorted, as she stepped back to close her door.

Clearly my hopes were not to be realized. I flipped a wave and went out the front door, depressed at my failure to learn anything at all. In whodunit novels, the suspects fall all over themselves trying to blurt out information to the amateur detective. Fiction!

I arrived at the Twiller house and was admitted by Camille. The living room was swollen with faculty people, administrators, and neighbors. The gardener had been pressed into service as a bartender in one corner. I squirmed through the crowd, murmuring polite noises, and waited for a drink. I had to pinch myself in order to avoid staring at the boy's hands for signs of soil under his fingernails. A whimsical theory, at best. Poor Mildred would not have had a tea party with the gardener.

Clutching my drink, I worked my way to a distant corner and studied the crowd for familiar faces. Britton hadn't mentioned whether he would succumb to duty and come, but he wasn't there yet. Maggie was home; that much I knew. I remembered that she had said she was expecting a visitor, and I wasted a few idle brain cells thinking about that. The scotch would do in another chunk. A few more went to wondering at what age I was apt to become a vegetable.

Douglas drifted past with the department chairman, engrossed in conversation. He gave me a quick nod, but steered his captive toward a sofa. Business before pleasure.

I wandered a few feet from my post to engage in appropriately subdued dialogue about poor Mildred, but I realized that I was again garnering smirks from those who had read the damnable book. Apparently everyone in the room, I concluded as I edged out of the living room. I considered standing in the foyer, dismissed the idea, and retreated to the den to practice disdainful looks.

I shut the door. As I turned around, I noticed a two-drawer filing cabinet. No tacky metal furniture for the Twillers; it was of a rich mahogany with antique brass pulls. I bent down to run my hand over the wood. A little square of paper was taped on each drawer, the handwriting spidery and timid. Mildred's.

The first drawer was devoted to contracts and royalty statements. The second drawer purported to contain current notes and research. My nose twitching, I opened the drawer to see if I might find any notes about *Professor of Passion,* specifically ones mentioning the Carlton character. Mildred had wanted to explain, I told myself in a self-righteous voice as I dug through the files. I would give her the opportunity to do so, albeit posthumously.

I found the file and slipped it out. With a nervous glance at the closed door, I sat down on the sofa and opened the file. My jaw fell against my chest. There were a dozen or so sheets of paper covered with handwriting, but the handwriting in no way resembled the spidery formations on the drawer labels. The words sprawled aggressively across the pages, bold and unmistakably masculine. Douglas's.

The words refused to come into focus as I goggled at them. Why had Douglas written notes for his wife? Or had he? I squinted until I could make out the writing. Possible titles, snippets of prose, a few similes that had caught his fancy. I shuffled through the pages to search for Carlton's name. Britton's name leaped off the page, followed by his academic background, his physical description, and a date from ten years ago. A doctor's name and an obscure medical phrase or two. A girl's first name—Jeanne—underlined by a heavy slash. A series of exclamation marks in the margin.

Stunned, I sat and stared at the information that had been compiled with the precision of a bureaucratic mind. Not Mildred's—or even Azalea's—mind, however; this was clearly Douglas's work. But why?

The doorknob rattled. I gulped back a shriek and shoved the file under a throw pillow as the door opened. I looked up to find Lieutenant Rosen's feral grin in all its glory.

"Oh," I managed to choke out, "it's you."

His eyes shifted to the pillow beside me. "It is I," he agreed genially as he moved forward. Before I could sense his intentions, he snatched up the pillow.

We both stared at the file.

"What's that?" I said, trying to appear properly shocked.

He chuckled at my ingenuous expression. "Why, Mrs. Malloy, whatever could that be? I do believe it is a file, perhaps from that very cabinet. Do you think Mr. Twiller would mind if I glanced through it?"

I gave up the ingenue routine and grabbed the file. "Sit down and read," I said briskly, "but you'll have to go second. I had it first, Lieutenant Rosen."

He gave me a reproachful look. "Is that any way to talk to the head of the Farberville CID? I agree that it lacks the reputation of Scotland Yard, but we do our best."

For the moment, I had almost forgotten the roles. I turned on what charm I could rally, batted my eyelashes, and cooed, "I don't quite know, Lieutenant. I've never been suspected of strangling anyone before."

"First time for everything," he said blandly as he sat down and pointed at the top page of the papers in the folder.

Unable to produce anything remotely adequate in response, I settled back and began to read.

SEVEN

When I finished the final page, I tossed the folder in Lieutenant Rosen's lap and propped my head on my hands. "Oh, my God," I muttered to myself, struggling to accept what I had read—in Douglas's handwriting.

The lieutenant scanned the page, straightened the papers, and closed the folder. He returned it to the cabinet, then came back to the sofa and sat down.

"Fascinating stuff," he said in a cheerful voice. "Nothing a detective likes better than names, dates, and verification. So neat and tidy, compared to the normal hodgepodge of information. It looks as if I might need to speak to a few people once more."

"I presume I'm one of them," I said flatly. I had just read all the details of Carlton's involvement with the coed, from the initial dalliance under the seminar table (dusty but creative) to the standing reservation at the Motel D'Amore (pure sleaze) on the highway. Times, dates, and even the course (Italian Renaissance Prose) the girl was taking from Carlton. Everything but her name, rank, and shoe size.

Lieutenant Rosen shrugged and said, "I knew most of the information about your husband. The police officers did a bit of background before they closed the file."

"Did you know all of that before you questioned me last night?"

"Jorgeson filled me in," he admitted, grinning. "However, I haven't received anything on Blake and Holland yet. I suspected that the oblique references carried some truth, but your snooping has saved me quite a bit of time, Mrs. Malloy."

"You're welcome. Anything to crucify a friend."

He leaned back and crossed his legs, as if we were settling in front of the television set to watch "Masterpiece Theater." "Now, you may be jumping to conclusions. Twiller does seem to have the information confirmed, but he might have made it up, for all we know. I'd prefer outside confirmation before I plug in the electric chair and test the switch."

It was not the moment for levity. Glaring, I said, "You may be right. Britton swore that the whole insinuation was pure fantasy and that he simply resented his name appearing in such a book. I told him that I believed him."

"Did you?"

"Of course, I did! I've known him since he came to Farber over ten years ago. He's not the sort to—" I couldn't get the damning words out in a controlled voice.

"Pressure a fifteen-year-old into having an abortion to save himself from a statutory rap?"

"Exactly. Britton is a kind, gentle man. The undergraduates wrestle each other during registration to get into his classes. He's not the sort to be involved with some Lolita with a punk-rock haircut."

"The names and dates are in the file. I'll know in a day or so if the charges were actually filed or if it is, as you believe, pure fantasy."

"He's nice, charming, erudite, sincere," I insisted obstinately.

"And single."

"And single." I curled my lip at the insufferable man. "I don't fool around with married men. Like policemen, they're excruciatingly egotistical."

"Admirable, Mrs. Malloy. You may be the only one within the Farber English department with any scruples. When do these people find time to teach?"

"Carlton hardly ever missed a class," I began hotly. The heat evaporated, however, and I added, "Office hours seem to present a lot of opportunities for intimacy with the students, I suppose. From what we read, the dean would be a bit startled to find out what goes on in his ivy towers."

"Or in Miss Holland's living room," he said with a distracted expression. Suddenly he grabbed my hand and pulled me to my feet, ignoring my astonished yelp. The door flew open. I gazed into Douglas Twiller's narrowed eyes.

"Claire? Lieutenant? I was wondering where the two of you slipped away, but I certainly did not expect to find you here." Douglas came into the den. Although he was making a pretense of genteel bewilderment, his eyes flickered to the filing cabinet.

Lieutenant Rosen jabbed me with his elbow. Swallowing a second yelp in less than half a minute, I said, "Oh, Douglas, I know it's silly, but I was overcome with emotion and came in here to compose myself. The lieutenant came in only a minute ago to—er, see if I needed a glass of water."

"Water, Claire?" Douglas's right eyebrow rose, a nifty trick I had yet to master. "I thought you preferred scotch in a crisis."

"It's a minor crisis. I'll help you to the water," Lieutenant Rosen said. He caught my elbow and tugged me past Douglas. We wiggled through the crowd until we reached the kitchen.

Camille stared at him as he hunted through cabinets for a glass. "Can I be of assistance?" she said.

He shook his head and kept up the clatter. After he had found a glass, he filled it at the tap and offered it to me. "Drink this, Mrs. Malloy."

"Thank you," I said between sips, hoping the urge to giggle would drown if I didn't choke.

Camille snorted and waltzed out of the kitchen with a newly stocked platter of canapés, clearly unimpressed with our childish antics. I put down the glass before the water sloshed onto the floor. "I feel like my hand was found in the cookie jar. Why didn't you tell him what we discovered, instead of meekly scuttling away?"

"I intend to discuss the file with Twiller, but I think we ought to wait until his guests are gone. He seems to be enjoying the solicitude—and it is his hour of glory."

"Those research notes were in his handwriting. We deserve an explanation," I said. I suspected that I knew what he would say—but I wanted to hear it from him. Poor Mildred, I thought with a sigh.

The lieutenant and I eventually rejoined the wake. Douglas gave us a few peculiar looks, but managed to stay on the opposite side of the room. Lieutenant Rosen was briskly absorbed by a circle of faculty wives, so I left him and wormed my way to the bar. Scotch is indeed better in a crisis; I don't even like the taste of water.

While the last guests were escorted to the door, Lieutenant Rosen and I moved to the center of the living room. Douglas came back in, stopped as he saw us, and let out a groan. "I don't suppose you're here for a nightcap?" he said wearily.

The lieutenant pointed to a chair. "Sit down, Mr. Twiller. It's time for a discussion—and it's apt to take a while. You look exhausted."

Douglas did as suggested, and he did look tired. Deflated, gray, perhaps even ill, I realized in surprise. I almost felt a twinge of sympathy, until I remembered the folder. Vicious, nasty stuff about people he supposedly cared for. I began to simmer, but quietly so that I would not be banished to the nursery in disgrace.

"We found the research file for *Professor of Passion,*" said Lieutenant Rosen. He looked down at the slumped figure in the armchair. "Mrs. Malloy and I had no problem identifying the handwriting. Yours, Mr. Twiller. Any comments?"

When Douglas shook his head, he continued, "The contents of the file were of great interest, too. According to those present at the reception, you averred several times that your wife could explain the insinuations about the Farber English faculty, past and present. How could she, Mr. Twiller—when she hadn't even read the book?"

Douglas seemed to toy with several responses, but at last discarded them. In a dull voice, he said, "She was shocked and went home to read the book. No migraine; nary a bout of sobs. Those were excuses. She was—ah, upset with the revelations."

"And you're Azalea Twilight."

"Mildred was Azalea Twilight," he protested. "She adored the opportunity to swoop around the country, being eccentric and wickedly romantic. Mobbed at the airport, awarded all sorts of nonsense. It was her life. But she couldn't write her name with a crayon, much less crank out two or three manuscripts every year."

"You could, and, in fact, did." Lieutenant Rosen sat down on the arm of a chair and studied Douglas as if he were a newly discovered species of carnivorous flora. Curious, but potentially dangerous.

"I seem to have a flair for it," Douglas said, flinching under the scrutiny. "I could finish a manuscript in under three weeks, which averages out to quite a bit of money per hour. Thousands, actually."

"But you passed it off as your wife's work."

Douglas glanced at me for sympathy. Finding none, he grimaced and said, "I have a reputation in academic circles, Lieutenant. Although you may be unaware of the back-stabbing that goes on among such people, I can assure you that it is more than common. If it were ever to be discovered that I wrote that—that genre of literature, then I would never again be published in any respectable journal. I would be a source of amusement for my colleagues, the object of crude remarks. My opinions would be dismissed as those of a crackpot. The chairmanship of the department would be out of the question."

"So Mrs. Twiller enjoyed the fame, and you enjoyed the money?"

"It was more than that. I rather savored the little deception, too. Knowing that all the world thought Mildred could write such lurid scenes, that she could even begin to produce the necessarily convoluted plots and forays into graphic ecstasy! It provided a great deal of secret amusement."

"I'm sure it did, Mr. Twiller. Regrettably, your wife was the one who was strangled because of your literary efforts."

"A terrible thing," Douglas said. "I'd prefer to rest now, if you're quite finished?"

"No, I'm not quite finished. About the contents of the folder? You seem to have done your homework on your colleagues, Mr. Twiller. It was enlightening."

"Was it? I'm delighted to have been of service."

"I was hoping you might explain why you spent such a tremendous amount of time and money on your research. A private detective agency, bribes to the registrar's office, all that tedious legwork."

Douglas licked his lips. "I simply decided to use more realistic characters, Lieutenant. Thus I studied those around me for inspiration, and later delved a bit into their histories to give myself a more rounded picture of them. My interest was purely from a technical standpoint; I had no personal interest."

"No, I don't think I can accept that," the lieutenant said. "Try again, Mr. Twiller—and do remember this is a homicide investigation, rather than a course in creative explanation. For instance, how did you find out about Carlton Malloy's female companion the night he was killed?"

"It was a wild guess."

"Come now, Mr. Twiller, no one is quite that astute when making a wild guess. Your account was a dazzling display of accuracy. You didn't miss a detail, from the bloodstained feathers to the car catching on fire after the companion had been moved to safety."

"I have a vivid imagination."

"And you're using it now."

"That is the truth, Lieutenant Rosen." Douglas stood up and started for the door. "I'm going upstairs to lie down. This inquisition has been a dreadful strain."

"I'm afraid I'll have to insist," Lieutenant Rosen said. When he realized that Douglas had no intention of stopping, he added, "Here, or at the station, Mr. Twiller; it's up to you."

Douglas snorted, but he did not stop. He went up the stairs, and shortly thereafter a door above closed with a quiet sound.

"You didn't strike much fear in his heart," I commented sweetly as I picked up my purse. "You ought to watch more cop shows on television. No one ever walks out on those guys."

"You watch too many of them. Witnesses are forever walking out on me, usually in the middle of a question," Lieutenant Rosen sighed. We let ourselves out and walked down the sidewalk to his car.

"Any theories?" he asked me.

"About the reasons for the libelous material in *Professor of Passion* or about the identity of poor Mildred's murderer?"

"Take your choice."

I wrinkled my nose. "Well, Douglas had very little reason to strangle Mildred. Now he won't be able to peddle his books under her name and stage presence. Azalea has died, too, and his career as an undercover pornographer is finished."

"So he had no motive to strangle his wife. On the contrary, he needed her alive and well."

"Mildred did mention that she might retire," I countered, shaking my head. "She confided to me at length over lunch last week. Shrimp salad and croissants. Coffee with cream.

However, she might have changed her mind after she had experienced anonymity for a few months. She certainly can't now."

The lieutenant opened his mouth but then snapped it closed, climbed into his car, and drove away. I stared at the brakelights as they flashed around the corner, feeling like Dorothy Gale from Kansas. A flock of munchkins would have been easier to handle than Lieutenant Rosen, I told myself as I walked toward my apartment.

It was after six, and darkness had settled in. Dry leaves blew across the sidewalk like arched spiders; a faint glow from behind the clouds promised the existence of a moon. Houses along the street looked warm and safe behind closed curtains. Murder was not a topic of conversation.

I enjoyed the solitude as I tried to sift through the information that had been thrust upon me—with a bit of my own help. Douglas Twiller, author of thirteen semipornographic novels, employing a private detective to provide fodder for his folder. And he wouldn't explain why, although he must have known a backlash was inevitable. And likely to prove expensive.

"Curiouser and curiouser," I muttered, squashing an errant leaf to hear the crunch under my foot. I wished Douglas could be dealt with as easily.

Mildred told me that she had intended to retire from the literary world. Douglas had avowed nothing but sympathy, but inwardly he must have panicked. But murdering her would not help; it rather tended to destroy whatever chance he might have in the future to persuade her to resume the Azalea role. He had suggested a vacation, a more civilized solution to bring her around.

The motive had to have arisen from the book. Someone too enraged to accept that the damage was already done had strangled the wrong person—an ironic twist of the silk scarf. Poor Mildred. We had all maligned her, and she hadn't even read the book. Poor, poor Mildred. No wonder she dashed out of the Book Depot like a terrified rabbit . . .

She deserved to be vindicated, but I had no idea where to seek a sacrificial goat. Douglas? Maggie? Britton? Or even Carlton, up from the grave to avenge his reputation? The whole thing was absurd; I did not drink cocktails with people who went around strangling people.

Caron was sitting on the couch when I arrived at the apartment. Her eyes were rimmed with red, her lip extended to its utmost degree of displeasure.

"Where's Inez?" I asked, trusting it to be a logical question.

"I don't know."

"Did you have a nice time at the pizza place?"

"Yeah. Just super."

"Did you have dinner?"

"I don't want anything."

"Neither do I, so we'll save the Lean Cuisines for another night. Do you have any homework?"

"No."

I abandoned the maternal efforts to elicit meaningful dialogue. I left her to brood and went into my bedroom to change into my robe. The scotch had not yet worked its way out of my veins, and my head was beginning to throb. I tried to find enough energy to investigate my daughter's latest pique, but instead went to the kitchen for a cup of tea. I heard a sniffle from the living room.

Caron came to the doorway, her arms wrapped around her shoulders. She looked younger than she had in years, and very vulnerable. "I think I know why you didn't want me to read the last Azalea book," she said. "It was about my father."

I fiddled with the teapot while I tried to decide how best to handle the subject. At last, feeling grossly incompetent, I settled Caron at the table and told her the whole story. We began with disbelief, moved through indignation, and finished with tears. She seemed to relax; perhaps the truth was more palatable than her doubts—or maybe she suspected that her father had never been as close to sainthood as his colleagues insisted.

"Why did Mildred Twiller put that in the book?" Caron asked. "That was cruel. I thought she was supposed to be a friend of yours. She must have known you'd figure it out."

Another sticky problem. I took a long drink of the tepid tea while I ran through my options. "We may never know," I said at last. I had no idea why Douglas had put the libelous material in the book; I suppose I thought that was close enough to the truth.

"She was your friend," Caron insisted. "She must have known that she would hurt you if she wrote about Dad and that—that girl."

"Mildred did say she had an explanation, but we'll never hear it. In the meantime, we'll just have to ride out the storm. There will be gossip at school, but I'd prefer that you not refute it with the same tactics you pulled on Rhonda Maguire. Smile contemptuously and walk away, Caron."

"Rhonda Maguire happens to be my dearest friend. She knew I was only kidding. It was all Inez's fault."

I choked on a mouthful of tea. "I thought you were defending your dearest friend, who is Inez."

"I hate Inez. She probably is a lesbian, and I have no intention of being stared at just because she doesn't date." Caron daintily wiped her nose on her sleeve and stood up.

"I think I'll call Rhonda and see if she wants to go to the library tomorrow after school. Good night, Mother."

I watched her leave, unable to think of a worthy reply. Caron and Inez were a team and, I had assumed, an unassailable one. What on earth could have happened? Five hours earlier they had been in the Book Depot, squabbling as usual but still the best of friends. Now Inez was out, and the unseen Rhonda Maguire in.

It was too intricate for me. I finished the tea and took a solid, dull, sexless biography to bed.

The following morning I dressed in drab, drank several cups of coffee, and prepared myself mentally for the funeral. Contrary to all the movie versions, the day was crisp and clear. After the customary and tedious ceremony at the church, a lengthy line of cars crept to the cemetery in the oldest part of town. We stood in a respectful circle as the minister intoned a few final words of comfort. The widower was gray about the face, but composed. An elderly relative bobbled beside him. Ashes to ashes, a handful of dirt, and we were free to go.

Lieutenant Rosen must have been lurking from a distance; he appeared by me as I walked to the curb. My car was wedged in; it would be several minutes before I could escape. He and I exchanged polite smiles as we leaned against the side of my car.

"Enjoy the show?" he asked mildly.

"Nothing more fun than interring a friend." I studied the bare branches of the trees. "Have you made any progress?"

"In a way. I received confirmation about Blake's unadmirable activities in Missouri. The story was still smoldering in a few back drawers, and the people there were willing to talk. It was true, Mrs. Malloy. The authorities were unable to make a case against him, but they had little doubt about his guilt."

"Oh." Brilliant. Since I had read the file, I had suspected as much. It still stung. For almost three years I had painted my toenails for the man. Pretended to appreciate the nuances of Hungarian wine. Put up with his beard. And slept with him.

Britton had not appeared at the funeral, despite protocol, and I wondered if he was busy submitting a resignation and packing up his wine collection. Maggie was likely to be similarly engaged. Abruptly I wished I were huddled under an umbrella to escape a cold drizzle; it would have been more suitable than the bright sunshine and cloudless sky.

"I guess I'll go back to the station," the lieutenant said, unperturbed by my lack of response. He shot me a broad grin. "A policeman's lot, and so on."

"Expecting more smut about the Farber faculty to come in on the teletype?" I snapped. "Are you checking to see if I left my grandparents buried in the basement?"

"Did you?"

"Dig it up and see, Sherlock." I fumbled through my purse for a tissue, standard equipment for any funeral. When I looked up, he was gone. The car parked in front of mine was not, however, and I could only seethe impatiently as I searched the dwindling crowd for someone who might be able to afford the shiny red Mercedes. Farber faculty people drove Japanese imports or used station wagons.

At last I perched on the hood to wait stoically, if not graciously. In the middle of composing a wisecrack to the Mercedes owner, I saw a figure slink behind an elm on the far side of the cemetery. Although I hadn't seen the face, I recognized the slumped posture.

I hopped down and jogged across the grass. When Inez

saw me, she broke into a jerky lope among the tombstones and memorial statues, leaping over a few with surprising agility.

"Inez!" I called, flabbergasted by her actions. "Come back here, or I'll—" I couldn't think of a suitable threat in my gaspy condition, so I settled for a glower potent enough to bring one of the cemetary residents to his feet. The only response was an increase in velocity.

Inez reached the gate and headed down the sidewalk toward a row of shops. I knew that I looked like a rabid child molester as I raced after her; my eyes were still glowering and my mouth distorted from the effort. I shouldn't have dropped my aerobics class, I told myself in a tortured tirade.

Finally Inez yielded to what she must have thought the inevitable, since she couldn't hear my death rattle. Clutching her purse to her chest, she stopped and waited for me to catch up with her. Her face was carved of the same marble as the stones she had leaped over, cold and impenetrable.

"Why on earth did you run away from me?" I managed to gasp.

"I didn't run away, Mrs. Malloy. I didn't want to be late for fourth period, that's all. I have office duty third period, and I just sort of slipped out of school for the funeral." She tried to sound earnest, but we both knew she was lying. I wondered why.

"I'll drive you back to the school, Inez," I said firmly, grabbing her arm in case she decided to try another sprint. The child was a damn gazelle, I thought as I pulled her back toward my car. One more effort like that and I could have checked right into the cemetery for a plot of my own.

"So you're AWOL from school?" I said, with the voice of a sympathetic confidante rather than of a parent, I hoped.

"Only office duty and lunch. It doesn't matter."

"And you were determined to attend Mildred's funeral?"

Inez slithered out of my grasp and stuffed her hands in her pockets. Her purse thudded against her thigh as she hurried up the hill. A flush crept up her neck. Breathless but determined, I willed myself not to beg for a rest and caught up with her. I repeated my question.

"I had to, Mrs. Malloy," she answered solemnly. Behind her thick lenses, her eyes glistened. "It was for Azalea. I asked Caron to come with me, but she said she couldn't miss algebra without getting caught. She could have, though. I would have paged her from the office and said there was an emergency at home."

"Caron wouldn't come to the funeral with you?" That was not a surprise. Azalea had slipped in Caron's popularity poll.

"No," Inez sniffled. "She doesn't want to talk about poor, departed Azalea, and she said she didn't even want to read her books anymore. I wrote the eulogy for the school newspaper all by myself. I'm the only one who cares about Azalea Twilight."

"Caron does change her mind," I said. "Did she tell you about it?"

"No. She just said that stuff about missing algebra."

"Will you tell me why you ran from me, Inez?" I asked gently. Deviously, but gently. I would have patted her shoulder if I could have kept up with her at the same time, but I needed my last bit of energy to climb the hill.

Inez shrugged but remained silent. We arrived at my car without further discussion. The Mercedes had disappeared. I put Inez in, went around, and climbed into the driver's side. Inez's behavior earlier mystified me. I was not, after all, a truant officer with a net. The girl had spent a goodly portion of her adolescence in my living room; she was not usually terrified by my attractive face and kindly demeanor.

"Did Caron say anything about why she refused to go to the funeral?" I persisted as we pulled away from the cemetery. There were about twelve blocks to manipulate the conversation. I unobtrusively slowed to a steady ten miles per hour.

"No. She just doesn't want to talk to me anymore. She thinks I'll tell the police what we did Sunday—" Inez slapped her hand over her mouth and ducked her head, but I had seen the look of terror flash across her face.

"What would you tell the police?" I steeled myself not to overreact, despite the sudden icy clutch of fear in my stomach. "You and Caron aren't exactly juvenile delinquents, after all. The police aren't interested in silly pranks." Dear God, let her giggle, I added to myself. An exercise in futility.

"I can't tell you," Inez groaned.

"You and Caron saw something Sunday?" I watched her out of the corner of my eye as I tried to make sense of her chopped sentence. It took only a block, but by now I had slowed to a turtlish creep. "Inez, does this have anything to do with Mildred Twiller's murder?"

"Not really, but Caron said—never mind, Mrs. Malloy."

She folded herself up and refused to speak, in spite of my barrage of pleas and dark threats. I dropped her off at school, watched until she was safely through the door, and then, my fingers white on the steering wheel, drove home.

EIGHT

I sat on the sofa and brooded for a long time. Mildred murdered by someone I might know. My erstwhile lover with a decidedly ugly blot on his record. My daughter withholding information from the police. Most likely the information had nothing to do with high school pranks or library fines. As distasteful as it was, I had to admit that Caron might know something about Mildred's death. It was one thing to hope I wouldn't be imprisoned for the crime; I certainly wasn't going to allow it to happen to my offspring, in spite of her proclivity for melodrama.

It seemed like the moment had come to stop wandering about aimlessly, motivated by nothing more than vague curiosity. Neither Inez nor Caron was apt to tell me whatever they felt was so vital, but perhaps I could find out myself. One step ahead of Lieutenant Peter Rosen, who might not feel the stirrings of maternal instincts.

I went into Caron's room to see if the Azalea series had

indeed been discarded. The designated bookshelf, normally decorated with scented candles and plastic flowers, was empty. It had even been dusted, which was not only a miracle but also an act completely alien to her character. Caron is not a sanitary soul; she could scrape up the material under her bed and submit it as a science project. And win a blue ribbon.

I found the books in the trash can in the kitchen. Delicately digging through the damp coffee grounds, I took the books out, wiped them off with a paper towel, and spread them across the kitchen table. There were twelve, but the final opus, *Professor of Passion,* was not among them.

I left them and went to my bedroom. My copy, still half-read, was on the bedside table. Derek glinted at me, but I put my mug on his face and sat down on the bed. This copy had come from the carton behind the counter. The one I had purchased, complete with purple flourish, had vanished sometime during the reception. Not a tragedy of any magnitude, but annoying.

Almost everyone at the reception had bought one of them, peer pressure being as potent in academic circles as it is in junior high schools. There had been one on my desk at one point, I remembered with a frown, but it too had vanished. I wondered if there was any way to count up the copies that had been sold—or if there was any reason to do so.

A peculiar thought entered the mental muddle. I had been honored with the first copy of the damn thing, and everyone who came into the Book Depot had been awarded a similar honor. But Maggie Holland had been clutching a copy as she marched across the sidewalk at the head of the demonstrators. Minutes later she had stormed in to take the center ring. Where had she gotten her copy?

Nancy Drew did not garner fame by sitting on her bed wrinkling her forehead. I went downstairs and knocked on Maggie's door. I was gratified to hear footsteps cross the living room. The door opened to a cautious slit.

"Claire." Not a warm welcome, but she did get the name out without visible agony.

"Hello, Maggie," I said as I nudged her aside and went into the living room. "I didn't see you at the funeral this morning."

"I wasn't there." Maggie closed the door and leaned against it, watching me with a pinched expression. She was dressed in her typical array of army surplus, bargain basement, and rummage sale. Politically correct, I presumed, but a bit baggy. Khaki was not her color. It tended to clash with her sporadic splotches.

"I would have thought propriety demanded your presence, what with Douglas destined to head the department and all," I said. I dug my heels into the carpet and ordered my feet to sprout roots.

"I submitted my resignation this morning. It seems the regents met last night to discuss the potential threat to Farber's pristine reputation. The dean called afterward to suggest I slip away quietly."

"Oh, Maggie, I'm sorry," I murmured. "I suppose that Mildred's book has done a lot of damage to us all. Farber is not the most liberal of liberal arts schools, but don't you think you could—"

"What do you want, Claire? I'm in the middle of packing, and I need to make some copies of my résumé to send off before the gossip seeps across the western hemisphere. At this point I'm praying for a backwater junior college to at least read my résumé."

She spoke softly, but there was a venomous edge to her voice that hinted at impending fury. I decided to push on before the fireworks started—and someone got burned.

"I wanted to ask you a question."

"The question being: Did I strangle Mildred Twiller? No, I'm sorry to say that I didn't have the opportunity. If I had been there, who knows what I might have done." She looked at her taut fingers.

"No, of course not, Maggie," I said hastily. "I was wondering where you found your copy of that—that nasty book? It occurred to me that you never came into the Book Depot to buy one, and I didn't notice anyone leaving once the champagne fountain started to bubble."

"I told that policeman about it. An anonymous donor."

"That's odd, Maggie. The books came in cartons, and they weren't opened until Mildred arranged a display. Who could have sent you the copy?"

"What difference does it make?"

"I don't know." I didn't, for that matter.

Maggie glowered, visibly battling with herself to remain under control. "I have no idea who sent me that book, but if I ever find out, I'll gladly tell you. Perhaps I can send you a postcard from my new post in Greenland, if I'm lucky enough to find one there or anyplace else. Good-bye, Claire."

I obediently edged toward the door. "Did it come in the mail?"

"It appeared in my mailbox Sunday about noon, in a plain brown wrapper. Unmarked." She reached for the doorknob. "Good-bye."

I stopped in the doorway. "Where's your copy now?"

"I considered having it bronzed, but changed my mind. I don't know where it is—and I really don't care. Look around your store for it if you want a souvenir of my swan dive into academic obscurity." A hand shoved me into the hall, and the door slammed inches from my nose. My hair fluttered in the breeze.

I stood in the foyer for a moment, chewing on my lip as I tried to visualize the scene at the reception once Maggie had finished her selected readings. Mildred's exit, the expectant faces awaiting bloodshed, the awful confrontation with Douglas . . . Maggie had come up behind me to bellow at Douglas—and had shoved the book at him.

Seconds later he had gone to my office to call Mildred to see if she had arrived home safely. Maggie's copy, ergo, was the one left on my desk. Then, undoubtedly influenced by the human conduct that seemed prevalent that day, it had vanished. But my office is not the most organized place; perhaps the book had fallen on the floor and had been kicked under something or into a corner. It might be there, and it might have some clue to its origin.

And it might not be worth a Confederate dollar, I warned myself as I went upstairs to get my purse and keys. The Book Depot was officially closed for the day in a gesture of respect. However, that was no reason not to slip in and hunt for Maggie's copy of *Professor of Passion*. It was preferable to sitting on the sofa worrying about Caron's foray into felony.

I hurried down Thurber Street and let myself in the store. Sunlight spilled into the front room but left in a huff when I closed and locked the door behind me. The building had few windows, and the ones it did have were too high to be cleaned more than once a year. My office had no windows at all. I put my hand on the light switch, then dropped it and went on.

The shelves were dim, misshapen structures that reminded me of the tombstones in the cemetery. I forced myself to listen to the cars rumbling down the street in a haze of carbon monoxide. It was the middle of the afternoon, after all. Hardly a midnight drama with a vaporous, chortling shade and a distant rattle of chains from the attic.

There was more than enough light to move down the center aisle to the office. I knew I was behaving like a gothic novel heroine, allowing myself to imagine the worst in the shadows. Old buildings make noises; there was no reason why mine shouldn't shudder occasionally. Perhaps the cockroaches were throwing a party or the rodents plotting a revolution. I would catch them in little army jackets, identical to Maggie's, and they would throw up their paws in panic. Their maps, drawn on the insides of match covers, would—

A chair squeaked in the office. The squeak was loud, unmissable. Not even in my fantastical ravings could I envision rat revolutionaries large enough to produce that squeak. I sucked in a gulp of air, my foot poised in midstep and my fingernails cutting into my palms. Nancy Drew was better at this, I thought as I stood and gaped at the darkness at the end of the aisle. She prowled ahead, undaunted by the possibility of danger. I, on the other hand, felt that a silent retreat and a quick call to the police would be more seemly for a woman my age, who had every intention of having more ages in the future, including that referred to by Madison Avenue as the Golden Years.

I tried to convince myself that I had heard one of those antique sounds I had been smiling about seconds earlier. Broad daylight outside, a Tuesday afternoon in Farberville, throngs of people on the sidewalk. It was not a castle in Bavaria; it was my very own musty bookstore.

It took several minutes of mental dialogue to get my foot back on the floor, but I did. Squaring my shoulders, I prowled ahead. I admit there was a slight tremble to my hand as I opened the office door, but I had resumed breathing, which I felt was a minor triumph. My lungs refroze as a figure stood up behind the desk.

"I thought that might be you," said Lieutenant Rosen.

"What the hell do you think you're doing?" I demanded when I could trust my voice.

"Same thing you're doing, I would imagine. But I'm glad you came by; it was getting a little boring in the dark by myself."

"Do you have a search warrant?" I knew there was a reason why I read all those police procedurals.

His white teeth glinted in the darkness. "I didn't search anything. To the best of my knowledge, judges don't issue sit warrants."

"Would you please explain what you're doing here? Then, if it's not too much trouble, I'd like to know how you got in and when you're leaving!" I was rather proud of myself for the show of indignation, since my knees had turned to Jell-O and my heart to whipped cream topping.

"Sit down, and I'll answer at least two of your questions." He switched on a penlight and escorted me to the chair across from the desk. "Now," he said genially, when he was back at his post, "I would suspect you've been trying to find a copy of the book that stirred up all the trouble. Miss Holland's, to be more precise. She doesn't know where it came from or where it went, which is puzzling."

I numbly repeated the earlier conversation with Maggie,

inwardly despising the man for the superior expression I couldn't see in the darkness. I admitted I had come to search the office for the copy and was sweetly informed that it was not there.

"You searched!" I accused him, jabbing a finger in his general direction.

"I looked around. You could have misplaced a herd of buffalo in this room and not found it for years, Mrs. Malloy. Have you ever considered using some sort of filing system?"

I considered a few tart replies but bit down on my lip and sulked for a few minutes. "Then where do you deduce the errant copy is, Sherlock? Do you think the buffaloes ate it?"

"I have no idea," he said cheerfully, "but I'm hoping someone else is equally concerned about it. Concerned enough to come looking for it here, while the store is closed and its proprietor safely at home where she belongs."

Protected by the darkness, I made an unladylike gesture at him and said, "I am where I belong. If you suspect someone is going to skulk around my store and search my office, then I prefer to be here. If you don't like it, get a warrant."

For the first time, he sounded a bit churlish. "I wish you'd leave, Mrs. Malloy. A visitor might not appreciate my surprise."

"I wish none of this had happened, but that hardly alters the situation, does it?" I crossed my legs and tried to find a comfortable position in the upright chair. There wasn't one. After resolving to buy a new chair, I resumed the conversation. "So, whom do we suspect?"

"Well," he said, giving in gracefully, "I told you that Britton Blake is not the white knight you had assumed. Margaret Holland has also been investigated, and it seems that Twiller's notes are for the most part accurate. That, coupled with the references to your husband, does provide a motive or two."

"Three." Even I can add.

"Three. We've also been checking on some others, including the maid and the gardener. They both appear to be what they claim: graduate students in need of a job. No one saw the maid at the library, but she has a pile of reference cards to back up her story. The gardener, when pressed, admitted he had been drinking beer with some friends instead of cleaning the flowerbeds. His story is confirmed, and I imagine the maid's will also be confirmed."

"What about Douglas?"

"We pressed him, and he finally yielded. It seems he drove directly to an apartment complex on the other side of the campus. He claims one of his students needed to revise a paper and had requested help. He didn't want to involve the student, unless it was necessary. Chivalry thrives in Farberville, apparently."

"The student has blond hair and a closetful of miniskirts, right?" I sighed, remembering Douglas's vow of innocence. On the other hand, I added judiciously, he had said one affair was over; he simply hadn't mentioned that a new one had sprung into existence.

"The girl agrees that he was there from three-thirty until almost seven o'clock helping her with her paper. He went home to find the police cars in front of the house. A busy day, but all of his time has been accounted for."

The chair squeaked, but I couldn't tell what he was doing. Loading his gun, I thought with a twinge of nervousness. At least he had no idea about Caron and Inez. I was still one step ahead.

"Is there any estimate of the time when poor Mildred died?" I asked.

"Between three o'clock, when she was last seen, and four-thirty, when her body was discovered," Lieutenant Rosen answered in his cheerful voice, not sounding the least bit daunted by the vagueness. "Miss Belinski was quite firm about the time she arrived at the Twiller house. She said she stared at the kitchen clock the entire time she talked to you, and it etched itself on her mind."

"So you've made almost no progress on the case. I should have called Scotland Yard, even with the transatlantic rates so high."

"Not true—" He broke off, and even in the darkness I could sense his body tensing as he rose to his feet.

"What?" I whispered, staring about with no success. "Did something crawl up your leg?"

"Shhh. I heard a noise."

"I didn't hear anything," I protested in a hiss. I was beginning to feel like a teapot, but I was alarmed by his actions.

"Shhh. Sit there and don't move, no matter what happens. Someone is outside the back door." He tiptoed across the floor and crouched in the corner behind the door.

I did as ordered, but after several minutes the routine grew tedious. I hadn't heard anything, and I was not about to sit and hold my breath indefinitely. Although, I admitted to myself, it seemed that Lieutenant Rosen had no need of oxygen.

When I was about to suggest he take a tiny breath, the door opened. A flashlight flooded into my eyes, dazzling me as if it were a hundred-carat diamond. I put my hands on my eyebrows and tried to blink away the glare. "Who is it?" I snapped.

The light whipped across the room as the lieutenant came from his corner with the determination of a rejuvenated boxer. Contact was made. The two bodies, entwined like amorous octopi, began to stagger around the room, thudding and stomping, grunting and growling, careening into furniture. I could see arms, legs, shoulders, and a few jabbing elbows, but no faces. The beam of light darted across the ceiling and back in a frenzy of indecision.

As amusing as the scene was, it too began to pale. I reached over my shoulder and switched on the light. Then, bright with curiosity, I sat back to watch the rest of the show.

Lieutenant Rosen and Douglas Twiller slowed down as they noticed the light. Finally, with a few parting snarls, they pushed away from each other and retreated to their respective corners. Their faces were both scarlet, their mouths both twisted and wet, their eyes glazed by the sudden light. They panted in unison.

"Douglas, what are you doing here?" I asked, when he seemed to have begun a recovery. The lieutenant made a rude noise at me, but I ignored him and kept my eyes on Douglas.

"Claire, Lieutenant Rosen," Douglas murmured, nodding to each of us. "I must say I didn't expect to find you sitting here in the dark. Very peculiar of you."

It was eerie, this repetition of the conversation we had had previously in his den. Lieutenant Rosen raised his eyebrows at me, then came out of his corner. "Were you looking for something, Mr. Twiller? A stray copy of *Professor of Passion*, perhaps?"

"How perceptive, Lieutenant. I came by to pick up the carton of unsold books," Douglas said with dignity. Despite the tone, it was almost a question.

"And let yourself in the back door with a key you had accidentally pocketed the day of the reception?"

Douglas slapped his forehead in mock dismay. "So that's how it happened to find its way into my pocket! I've been worried about that since Sunday afternoon, although I did find it fortunate. Here, Claire, you must need this more than I." A key clattered onto the desk.

I admired the effort. No admission of anything more damning than a bout of absentmindedness. "Thank you, Douglas," I said softly. "You might have called so that I could have opened the store for you, if you truly needed the extra copies of *Professor of Passion*. Or asked me at the funeral."

The reference to the funeral deflated him. His hand fell to his side and he had the grace to look ashamed, though by no means guilty. "I didn't have a chance to speak to you at the funeral, Claire, since I had to deal with Mildred's great-aunt. She did so dodder. Later, I didn't want to disturb you with my petty mission."

"That won't work, Douglas," I said. "We're all here for the same reason: to find the copy of the book that Maggie discovered in her mailbox Sunday. About noon, she told me. The cartons at the Book Depot were not yet opened at that time, and those were the only copies of *Professor of Passion* in Farberville. It couldn't have come with the shipment, yet she had it before the reception. I should have realized it had to be one of the advance copies and, therefore, a gift from the author."

The author began a protest, but I frowned him into silence. "The copy can be traced, Douglas; no doubt it's marked 'Advance.' You left it in the office by mistake and came today to look for it. But why sneak a copy to Maggie?"

Lieutenant Rosen cleared his throat. "I think I can answer that, Mrs. Malloy. It was necessary so that the actors would play their roles with precision. The entire script was written by Mr. Twiller some time ago, and the scenes unfolded exactly as he had hoped."

"Actors?" I said, my frown deepening.

"Actors," the lieutenant said firmly. "But of course they had no idea of the existence of the script—Mr. Twiller's little drama in three acts. First, he set up his wife as the victim by making tacit accusations in the book. Then, aware that Maggie Holland was preparing to lead the FWO, he slipped the advance copy into her mailbox before the reception. She discovered the libelous material and provoked the ensuing scene at the reception. Mildred went home to weep, everyone else stormed away with murderous expressions and lovely motives, and Mr. Twiller went home to strangle his wife."

Douglas gurgled and had to grab the edge of the desk to keep his balance. "Not bad, Lieutenant. But what about my alibi? I went from the Book Depot to the—the, er, tutorial session."

"Your wife was already dead by that time," he countered. He took a pair of professional-looking handcuffs out of his coat pocket and moved toward Douglas with a guarded expression.

Douglas's eyes widened and turned a metallic color that matched the handcuffs. "I stayed at the Book Depot until three-thirty. Claire will tell you that I was in her office on the telephone. I came out a minute or so after she returned."

They both looked at me. "I saw him go toward the office, but I can't swear that he stayed there. Maybe he went out the back door?" I said, oddly defensive.

Lieutenant Rosen paused to consider my suggestion, then

shook his head and said, "But you didn't see him on the railroad tracks. Miss Belinski was above you on Arbor, with a clear view of the street all the way to the end of the block. Even if he did slip out the back door, how could he have gotten to the house and back without being seen?"

"I don't know," I admitted darkly.

"Well," the lieutenant said, "Mr. Twiller does have a point. Unless you can figure out how he could have slipped past you and Miss Belinski, my theory won't hold up."

"Aren't you supposed to be the detective?" I sputtered. "Figure it out yourself, Sherlock—that's what you get paid for!"

The scene was unraveling at an alarming speed. I swung back and glared at Douglas Twiller, whose pallor had improved to a mottled cerise. "What about the book you left in Maggie's mailbox?"

"I left it there by mistake. I meant to put it in your mailbox; Mildred thought you might like to read it before the reception. I couldn't explain that I—I rather doubted that. But I didn't kill Mildred, Claire. She was my wife!"

"It wouldn't be the first time," the lieutenant cut in. We were all beginning to foam about the mouth, and I'm sure an observer would have called for the psycho squad to bring their nets. I would have welcomed them.

"Then why did you put that filth in the book?" I snarled at Douglas.

"I told you that I wanted more depth!"

"That's nonsense!" I shrieked.

"I can't help that!" he shrieked back.

"Then why did you steal the key so you could sneak into my bookstore? That seems pretty suspicious!"

"I came by to pick up the unsold books to take to the

bookstore at the mall. They've sold out and wanted all the copies they could get!"

"Oh, yeah?" I was running out of accusations. I glared at Lieutenant Rosen, who had the nerve to shrug in response. "Do something!"

"What?" he asked mildly. "I'm open for suggestions, but I'm afraid Mr. Twiller does have a legitimate argument."

"Just do something!" I turned my back on him to attack Douglas Twiller. But he was occupied with straightening his tie and checking to see that his jacket was buttoned. I swore to never, ever be involved with the male species again, no matter how persistent the hormonal pleas.

"I must run along," Douglas said, when the tie met his approval. "I'll pick up the unsold copies in a day or two, Claire—whenever you're open for business." He gave me the famous Twiller wink and strolled out the back door. Humming, for God's sake.

I heard a muffled sound behind me. I took a deep breath and turned around. "What's so damned funny?"

The lieutenant's chin trembled, but he shook his head and started for the front of the store. I dearly hoped he would trip over a display shelf and chip every one of his pearly white teeth. Every one of them. And I hoped his dentist was trained by the Marquis de Sade.

NINE

I went home again, motivated by a fanciful dream that I might find Caron there and eager to discuss whatever she and Inez had seen. She wasn't there. I heard no noises from downstairs, so I presumed Maggie wasn't there, either. People did seem to have an unnerving habit of not being handy when I wanted them—with the exception of Sherlock, who managed to be wherever I didn't want him to be.

I considered trying to finish *Professor of Passion* but couldn't find the necessary discipline for that distasteful a chore. Adverb-laden lust was unpalatable. It was time for action, if I could concoct something more strenuous than flipping pages or drinking tea.

Finally, I put on jeans and a turtleneck sweater, ruffled my hair into disrepute, and walked across the campus to the fine arts building to see if Sheila might be there. Nancy Drew, undercover agent, was on the prowl again—if no one noticed the crow's feet around my eyes or the sprinkling of gray hairs. After the events of the last few days, it was more of a deluge.

The classes were over for the day, but the studios were occupied by would-be Picassos and Rodins, slapping paint on canvases or chipping away at blocks of marble. Aside from their sporadic invectives, the building was peaceful.

I poked my head into all the studios and at last found Sheila in the pottery lab on the third floor. Her clothes were coated with clay; her hair was prematurely gray from the dust. She perched on a stool in front of a pottery wheel, intent on the pot that rose with mystical symmetry from the lumpish mass of clay. Her face glowed with satisfaction, and she looked surprisingly pretty.

I waited at the door until she noticed me. She sat back and took her foot off the treadle. Without her encouragement, the wheel whirled a few more times, then gradually stopped.

"Mrs. Malloy?" she said with a cautious inflection.

"Hello, Sheila. I came by to speak to you, but I'll wait if you need to finish the piece."

She rubbed her forehead, leaving a thick slather of clay. "No, I was about ready to quit for the day. If you don't mind, we can talk while I clean the wheel."

"It's about Mildred Twiller's death," I said. I came in and sat down on the corner of a scarred workbench. "The lieutenant doesn't seem to be making any progress on the case, and in the interim several of us are suffering. Do you know that Maggie has resigned?"

Sheila scraped up a handful of clay and threw it into a plastic garbage can. It disappeared with a glutinous, sucking sound. "Yes, she told me that it was inevitable once the board of regents heard about the book. She's not some kind of pervert, Mrs. Malloy; she has an unconventional sexual preference, but that doesn't make her an incompetent teacher—or a cold-blooded murderer."

"No one has accused her of that," I said, surprised. "She was at her lawyer's office during the time in question."

"It's just awful," Sheila said, avoiding my eyes. She scraped up the last of the clay, put it in the can, and found the lid. Then, subdued and clearly miserable, she leaned against the sink and stared at the straw-littered floor. "I wish I had never gone over there to look for Maggie. It's all my fault."

"Not precisely. Mildred's body would have been discovered in due time, and I suppose it would have given Douglas a heart attack if he had been the one. Luckily, he was involved all afternoon. He has an alibi of sorts."

"I heard he was just driving around."

"He was with a woman. It took him a while to admit it, but it seems he's in the clear. Between three and three-thirty, I was walking down the railroad tracks and didn't see him; you were above me on Arbor Street and didn't see him either." I gave her a chance to contradict me, but she merely picked a scrap of dried clay off her sleeve and flicked it to the floor. "You didn't see anyone else, did you?"

"I saw your daughter and her friend." She gave me an entreating look, as though in apology for the damning words.

"I saw them, too. They were on the bridge above the tracks," I said coolly. "That would have been about three-fifteen."

"No, I saw them earlier, just after you left the Book Depot. They were running down the street from the direction of the Twiller house, and they looked peculiar. I don't think they even noticed me, but not everyone does."

I forced out a laugh. "You don't mean to imply that they were actually in the Twiller house, do you? Two fourteen-year-old girls, strangling their most cherished author? That's absurd!"

"I wasn't implying anything of the sort, Mrs. Malloy. I don't even know that they had been in the Twiller house. They just came from there." Sheila blinked earnestly at me, and her throat rippled several times. She busied herself picking clay off the knee of her denim pants.

"Looking peculiar," I repeated grimly.

"Not peculiar, exactly. They were giggling madly and looking at something the skinny one had in her hand. Maybe they found a dollar on the sidewalk or something."

It was time to change the subject, I told myself in a thin, scared voice. Dr. Spock had never offered any advice on keeping one's child from being implicated in a felony. On the other hand, I hadn't read the most current edition. "If Maggie told you that she was going to her lawyer's office, why did you go to the Twiller house?"

"She was angrier than I've ever seen her. I went to her apartment to try to calm her down, but she wasn't there. Then the lawyer's service called to say that he would be on the golf course all afternoon and couldn't see her, so I . . . decided to stroll by the Twiller house."

"Maggie didn't go to her lawyer's office?" I struggled not to squeak. Bad memories. "Where did she go?"

"I didn't see her at all after the reception, and she wouldn't tell me afterward." Sheila dabbed at the corner of her eye with the tail of her shirt. A drop of moisture formed on the tip of her nose, and she blotted it before it could fall. "I went all over the campus trying to find her, but nobody had seen her. I wish I had gone home instead of going to the

Twiller house. I really do, Mrs. Malloy. I've caused trouble for everybody."

She certainly had. Now, her newest bit of observation had thrown Caron and Inez into the middle of things, which was the one thing I was trying to avoid. I wondered if she had mentioned it to Lieutenant Rosen, but I couldn't think of a prudent way to broach the matter. Maggie wasn't faring any better. If I hadn't sworn off murderous thoughts, I would have stuffed Sheila into her garbage can of clay. Less than charitable, but timely.

"Well, it's been enlightening." I stood up.

"I'm glad to know Mr. Twiller has been cleared, anyway," she snuffled. "He seems like such a kind man."

It did not reflect my personal sentiments, but I nodded and murmured a good-bye. When I left, Sheila was still leaning against the sink; it would be convenient if she burst into tears. From the expression on her face, it seemed a matter of seconds.

I walked back toward my apartment, but on a whim turned and went into Farber Hall. I knew the route to the English department on the second floor, having spent many an hour waiting for Carlton to escape a faculty meeting or to finish a seminar. Or what I now knew to be a tryst under the seminar table. I hoped he had the decency not to demonstrate his sexual prowess during an actual seminar; graduate students are always looking for an erudite role model.

The building was deserted. I listened to my footsteps as I climbed the first flight, lost in memories of fonder days. The office door was closed but not locked. I went inside and crossed to the wall where the boxes sat in tiers. Most of them had a few odd memos and letters; some had been neglected for days.

I looked for Maggie's name and found it above a

pointedly empty box. No memos for the scandalous Holland, I thought with a grimace. Britton's box was just above it, and it too had only a thin veneer of dust. It occurred to me that I hadn't seen him for a day or so. Knowing what I did about him, I felt no big loss, but a sense of guilt sent me to a secretary's desk to find a piece of paper.

After several minutes of effort, I tore up the paper and lobbed it into a wastebasket. There wasn't anything to say, I decided as I let myself out of the office and continued up the stairs to the third floor. The hallway was bleak, decorated with yellowed grade sheets from the previous semester and the flyers that promised overseas employment or assistantships at unfamiliar colleges.

The fourth floor was deserted as well. Carlton's office now housed a janitor, I noted without interest. If some poor, unsuspecting instructor was assigned that office, he would never comprehend the noises the ghosts might make. The moans would hardly be of the traditional sort.

I went back down and walked home. While I started the teapot, I tried to think of some way that Douglas Twiller might have murdered his wife, but I couldn't get past the fact that he would have been seen if he had gone home.

He had to be involved; the book was proof enough. He was acting as if he were guilty, damn it! He was my prime candidate, damn it! I wanted Britton and Maggie to be able to leave unobtrusively, to have the chance to find teaching positions somewhere else. Hardly anyone was hiring murder suspects these days. The interviews would be hedged with tactful questions about possible involvement: "Have you submitted any articles since you strangled your colleague's wife?"

I also wanted to get Caron and Inez out of the mess without any scars to their fragile, pubescent egos, if such a thing were possible. But I couldn't do anything until I knew what they had done. It looked grim. I looked grim.

Lieutenant Rosen looked grim when he knocked on the door in the midst of my second cup of tea. "I need to talk to you," he said, walking in as if he were welcome.

"Please come in," I said acidly to his back. "Did you drop by to raid the refrigerator?"

"Where's your daughter?"

"Studying with a friend." I couldn't get out a *why?* with a properly light tone, so I settled for a slightly bewildered smile as I took refuge in the kitchen.

"I've never seen her. I was wondering if she has your red hair and freckles." He wasn't.

"A fascinating topic for a police investigation, Lieutenant. I could find her yearbook and save you some time," I retorted. It was increasingly difficult to maintain the smile; I felt as though it might slip off my chin and splatter on the floor.

"Do you know where she's studying?"

I assumed she and Rhonda were at the Farber library, but I wasn't about to offer idle speculation. He was Sherlock; he could deduce her whereabouts without my help. "No, I don't. Is that all?"

"Then what about the friend with the meek expression? Do you have her address?" He wasn't smiling in response to my valiant efforts. He came up behind me, close enough for me to feel his breath on the back of my neck. "You're going to have to tell me, Mrs. Malloy. This is important."

"Why is it so important? They're a couple of typical teenage girls, for God's sake. They know absolutely nothing about any of this, and I won't permit them to be harassed because you can't find a killer!" I tried for an indignant tone, but I may have sounded a tad shrill.

"Douglas Twiller called the station a few minutes ago to report that his house had been burglarized, most probably Sunday afternoon. Your daughter and her friend were seen near the house. I need to speak to them."

I really ought to have put Sheila in the clay can, I told myself with a mental snarl. And fired up a kiln. The tawny lioness, protecting the wayward cub—it would have been a great defense. I might have made jurisprudence history.

"That's nonsense," I choked out, with a brittle noise that was supposed to be a laugh. "Caron and Inez are not burglars. Neither of them would dream of going into someone else's house, much less stealing something." And running down the street, staring at it in Inez's hand, while looking peculiar.

"Inez who?" he snapped, unimpressed with my logic. When I glared in response, he added, "Come on, Mrs. Malloy. If they were in the house—for whatever reason—then they might have seen someone there."

"They weren't there; they didn't see anything," I insisted.

"I want to question them. I don't understand why you're being so pigheaded about this!"

"You always bring out the best in me," I said, and stalked into the living room, leaving him to ponder that in private. By the time he came after me, I was on the sofa with a magazine in my lap. I looked up. "Are you still here? I thought I heard the door close."

His eyes were literally snapping above his white lips and jutting beak. If he'd had wings, he would have made a fine eagle—presuming the existence of a species with black, curly head feathers. His clenched fingers resembled talons, and I suspected his toes were curled as well. Fascinating imagery, but a little dangerous.

"I need to call the station." He wasn't asking permission, and I had no idea why he bothered to inform me of his intentions. He muttered into the receiver, his back turned. I visualized a knife cutting into the flat plane between his shoulder blades, which cheered me somewhat.

He made a surprised noise, glanced at me over his shoulder, and then began to whisper in an urgent voice. Although I strained, I could make out only a word or two of his conversation. It seemed to concern Douglas Twiller.

As he replaced the receiver, I snatched up the magazine and flipped through the pages with a pretense of interest in any of one hundred ways to redecorate a kitchen for under twenty dollars.

"Tell me where Caron is," he said harshly.

"I don't know, and I wouldn't tell you if I did," I answered, frowning at a photograph of café curtains made from tea towels. "Do you think these might look nice in my kitchen? I can make them for three dollars."

"I could arrest you for obstructing an investigation."

"I think blue might go better with the linoleum."

He balanced on the balls of his feet, looking as if he were on the verge of leaping at me. His mouth was twisted, his forehead creased with deep lines; it was an admirable display of fury tempered by self-control. I almost clapped to show my appreciation, but I didn't want to lose my place in the magazine.

"Is there something else?" I asked politely.

"Douglas Twiller is dead. He was found a few minutes ago, on the sofa in the den. He was strangled with a silk scarf. Now, will you tell me where your daughter is?"

"Douglas is dead? But that's absurd! He's a strong man—how could someone strangle him? That's impossible!" The magazine fell on the floor as I scrambled to my feet. My mouth continued to sputter at the same velocity, but I was barely aware of it. Douglas? Strangled? It was not a lovely picture.

Lieutenant Rosen gently pushed me back down on the sofa. "It doesn't take a great deal of strength to strangle someone from behind. Of course, you do have to be able to stand behind the victim and prepare a garrote. It would seem likely that Douglas Twiller trusted his murderer—or mistakenly underestimated the same."

"Who discovered the . . . ?"

"The maid, about ten minutes ago. Twiller called in the burglary about an hour ago, and Jorgeson was actually on his way there when the radio dispatcher contacted him. We'll know more when the coroner arrives." He crossed the room to stare out the window at Farber Hall. "As usual, we're having trouble locating our circle of interested parties."

"You don't think Caron—" I caught myself and took a deep breath. The idea was ludicrous, insane.

"Of course not! But I do think she saw something while she was in the Twiller house Sunday afternoon. Now, where is she?"

So much for the clever little game of evasion. I told him that she and Rhonda were at the Farber library, probably in one of the lounges where they could giggle without any dirty looks from the staff. I gave him Inez's full name and address. He made a quick call to the station, barked out instructions to have the girls collected, then tugged me to my feet and tossed me my coat.

"Where are we going?" I asked, stull stunned by the unexpected news of Douglas's death. A small voice from a corner of my brain was mentioning the fact that Douglas was no longer my best candidate for Mildred's murder. The voice was actually chortling, and I warned it to stop or risk a lobotomy.

"I need to go to the scene of the crime," he said, pushing me out the door. "In the meantime, I'm going to keep an eye on you until we locate your daughter. I don't want you to change your mind and try to warn her."

"I wouldn't do that," I sniffed. When he merely smiled, I added, "How did you find out she was near the Twiller house?"

"Miss Belinski called to say she had just remembered. It seems that someone jarred her memory. Good citizens do try to assist the police." Barbed, but cheerfully so.

"Then Miss Belinski ought to qualify for a gold medal," I said sourly. "But she told me that she didn't see Caron and Inez at the house; they were only coming from that direction. You're not even giving them the benefit of the doubt, you know."

He opened the car door for me, clearly uninterested in my thoughtful analysis. We drove the few blocks in silence. I tried to find an explanation for what had happened, but there didn't seem to be one that was at all credible. I had been so sure that Douglas was the murderer. He had, as Lieutenant Rosen suggested, choreographed the scene; he had to be the director. Now it seemed there was a second figure, whose identity was a total mystery.

The police cars were again parked in front of the gate, their blue lights reeling in the gloom of the late afternoon. My old friend, the supercilious teenager, watched me from his police car, looking not a bit surprised to see me in the lieutenant's custody—where he assumed I belonged.

We went into the house. The lieutenant left me in the foyer and followed Jorgeson to the den. Unable to stop my knees from quivering, I went into the living room and sat down. The ambulance attendants were there, with the same bored expressions. A regular class reunion, I told myself as I slumped into the cushions and closed my eyes.

"Hi," one of them said, undaunted by my inhospitable demeanor, "weren't you here last time? Is this your house or something?"

I opened one eye. "I have a thing about dead bodies. Every time I hear of one, I rush over in hopes of a glimpse. I'm thinking about signing up as an apprentice undertaker. Okay?"

"Sure, lady."

They moved to a far corner to whisper. I closed my eye and forced myself to think. Douglas had been killed within the last hour. I was at Farber Hall, creeping around by myself on some misguided notion that I could not explain. Maggie was out somewhere; I hoped she had an alibi for this one. I hadn't even seen Britton in a couple of days and therefore couldn't begin to imagine where he might be.

Lieutenant Rosen came out of the den. He gave some terse, unintelligible orders to the uniformed men, then beckoned to the ambulance attendants. The man with the black bag passed across the foyer. I waited. Jorgeson came to the doorway to stare at me, then popped out of sight. The front door opened, closed, and opened once again. Footsteps, more terse conversation, the squeal of the gurney's wheels on the porch.

The images flying through my head were too ghastly to entertain. I went to the liquor cabinet and poured myself two inches of scotch and then went to the kitchen to hide from the noises. Camille stood in the middle of the room, her shoulders curled and trembling.

She gave me a blank look and said, "What are you doing here?"

"I came with Lieutenant Rosen, Camille. Why don't you sit down in the dining room? I'll bring you a glass of brandy."

Her jaw flopped for a moment, but she finally nodded and slid through the door. I filled a tumbler and followed her to the dining room. After she had tossed off half the brandy, the color returned to her cheeks and the blank look was replaced with a certain slyness. Good old Camille was back.

"Are you under arrest, Mrs. Malloy?" she demanded, optimistically.

"No, Camille, I am not under arrest. The lieutenant was at my apartment when he heard about Mr. Twiller. You were the one who found the body, I hear."

"I came back from class about thirty minutes ago. Mr. Twiller hadn't touched the food I'd fixed for lunch, so I went to the den to see if he wanted a sandwich." She took a second slug of brandy, choked on it, and wiped her eyes. "He was on the sofa. At first I thought he was taking a nap, but when I went in, I saw a scarf cutting into his neck. The police pulled up just as I was running to the telephone to call them."

"It must have been terrible for you," I said soothingly. We sat and pondered the extent of the terribleness for a moment, which was, realistically speaking, quite a bit more terrible for Douglas than for Camille. "You must have been distraught, Camille. First Mrs. Twiller, then the burglary, and now this."

"What do you know about the burglary?" Her mouth tightened with suspicion, and she shoved the glass away as if I had served her a dose of amber cleaning fluid.

"I heard about it from the lieutenant. I'm helping him with the investigation, since I know all the people involved," I explained. If Lieutenant Rosen had heard that one, he would have laughed himself sick. However, he was safely tucked away in the den, doing whatever CID officers do in such situations.

Camille wasn't in on the joke. She was still wary, but eager to talk to someone. Although I surely wasn't her first choice of confidantes, she was stuck with me.

"Mr. Twiller mentioned it after the funeral," she said. "He told me someone had been in his wife's boudoir and had stolen a silver medallion she had been awarded by some romance group. She was very proud of it. He said he was going to report it as soon as he had the opportunity."

Oh, dear, I thought as I took a long drink of scotch. I had a fairly good idea who the guilty parties were—and so did Sherlock. "Was anything else missing?" I asked Camille. Something large enough to require a pickup truck or a moving van, I added in silent prayer.

"No, that was the only thing Mr. Twiller could determine had been stolen. He was sure it was there before they went to the reception Sunday; he said Mrs. Twiller decided not to wear it at the last moment, and he waited in the foyer while she took it back upstairs."

"Maybe it was stolen the next day?" I said. I crossed my fingers tightly enough to turn them into bloodless worms.

She shook her head, dissolving any hope I had left. "He noticed it was gone while the police were here that evening, but he was too upset to think about it. Mr. Twiller never made a mistake," she concluded in triumph, giving me the familiar smirk.

I stared at Camille, trying to envision her in the role of a strangler. She was slender, nearly anorexic. Her hands were white and unblemished; I suspected her housekeeping chores were done with negligence, if at all. And she didn't have a motive. She didn't even have a job anymore.

Reluctantly, I dismissed the idle dream of seeing her contemptuous expression disjointed by prison bars.

The answer lay in books and medallions, I decided as I finished the last few drops of scotch. Douglas must have been worried that the investigation was centering too closely around him. Once he had been confronted in my office and forced to admit he slipped the advance copy to Maggie, his only hope lay in shifting the attention. Unless he was innocent—which was absurd. He had called the police station to report the burglary, no doubt with the indignation of a homeowner returning from a vacation to a ransacked house. Then he had admitted a visitor, who knotted a scarf around his neck.

"Mr. Twiller finally made a mistake—a fatal one, at that," I said, sighing. Not a tender epitaph, but an accurate one.

TEN

Jorgeson took Camille away to get a statement. I went back to the living room, sat down, and willed myself to a sunny beach in the Caribbean, where my most pressing concern was the origin of my next drink. The palm trees were rustling above my head when Lieutenant Rosen found me. The beach receded, along with the balmy breeze, the muscular young men, and the aroma of rum flavored with fresh pineapple juice. The man simply didn't fit in.

"The uniforms picked up your daughter at the library. She's waiting at the station. Would you like to be present when she's questioned?"

"I was going to wash my hair, but since you were so kind to invite me, I suppose I might drop by the station," I said, with all the sarcasm I could muster. He failed to notice.

I followed him to his car—which was worse than mine, for the record—and we drove to the yellow brick building ringed by police cars. Business was brisk.

I had been there once before, when a cold-hearted meter maid had failed to appreciate that a certain parking meter was simply swallowing my coins without regurgitating enough precious minutes to have a prescription filled. The municipal judge had a pink nose and a kindly twinkle in his eyes, but it cost me five dollars anyway.

"Is Caron in a cell?" I asked as I eyed the row of vagrants and drunken Farber students on a bench across from the desk. With a rapist or a drug-crazed child molester? Sobbing under a lice-infested blanket? Withdrawn and too terrified to realize where she was?

"In the dungeon," Lieutenant Rosen said cheerfully, "strapped to the rack. We have a toddlers' size for children and a petite for juniors." He led me into a lounge filled with shiny plastic couches and vending machines.

Caron sat on one of the couches, a Coke in one hand and a half-eaten chocolate bar in the other. A young uniformed policeman was sitting next to her, enchanted by her winsome ways as she regaled him with the highlights of a high school football game. She was not overwhelmed to see me.

"Are you okay?" I demanded.

Caron produced a martyred smile for the young man, followed by a glare for me. Nostrils aquiver, she said, "Yes, Mother. I may get a bad grade in U.S. history, but I haven't been beaten with a rubber hose." We watch the same television shows.

"Did you call a lawyer?"

"I'm fourteen, Mother; I don't have a lawyer. I thought about calling the accountant, but I didn't have a dime."

I sat down beside her and patted her hand. It seemed properly maternal, if ineffectual. I stared across the room. "Well?"

Lieutenant Rosen nodded at the uniform, who promptly stood up and scurried away. Caron looked longingly after him but managed to pull herself together when the lieutenant sat down on the other side of her. He did not pat her hand.

"About your visit to the Twiller house," he began genially. "We've been wondering exactly what happened."

Caron stiffened. "How do you know about that? We didn't do anything wrong. We just wanted to see Azalea Twilight's boudoir while everyone was at the reception."

"You and Miss Brandon?"

"It was all Inez's idea, anyway. You ought to arrest her— I went along with her, but she's the one who—" Caron broke off, but there was a flicker of satisfaction on her face.

My daughter would not make a good spy; one Coke and she'd gladly recite her autobiography. A candy bar would produce my life story and probably my tax returns for the last decade, dubious deductions included. My accountant would commit suicide.

"Miss Brandon will arrive shortly," the lieutenant said, sounding as perplexed as I by her candor. "We've sent someone to her school to pick her up. Why don't you tell me exactly what happened, Miss Malloy? I can decide if it has any relevance to later events."

I felt as though I ought to do something, but nothing came to mind. I certainly couldn't tell Caron to shut up; the lieutenant would be less than delighted and Caron would seem guiltier than she was. If that were possible. I tried an expression that was meant to convey a stern message concerning discretion.

Caron shot me a quick frown that was meant to convey her embarrassment over my facial contortions. "I'll tell you everything if you want me to, Lieutenant. We were hanging around Sunday afternoon, trying to think of something to do. Inez wanted to sneak into the back of the Book Depot to get a glimpse of Azalea, but I figured Mother would see us and throw a fit. We walked around the neighborhood for a while, then Inez said we ought to walk past the Twiller house."

"And?" Sherlock was trying not to sound impatient.

"As we went past, we saw the maid leave with a stack of books. A few minutes after that, the gardener drove off. Since the Twillers were at the reception, we realized that the house was empty. Inez said we ought to sneak in for a quick peek, that nobody would ever find out. She said Azalea's boudoir was decorated in mauve and hot pink, because there was one exactly that color in *Tempestuous Dreamer*. I said that was silly, but Inez swore it was true."

Caron sat back, apparently satisfied that we now knew all the grisly details of her first escapade as a burglar. We stared at her, but she was already smoothing her hair in case the cute uniform was still in the station. I could see that she was wondering if she could pull out her compact to check her lipstick. She made a wise decision to leave her purse in her lap. I might have shoved the lipstick case down her throat, along with the compact and whatever else she had squirreled in her purse.

At last the lieutenant cleared his throat. "And you went into the Twiller house to—ah, test the hypothesis of the color scheme in the boudoir?"

"It wasn't mauve or pink; it was kind of a pearl white."

"A grave disappointment, I'm sure. While you were there, did you happen to hear anything or see anyone?"

She giggled. "We heard someone come in the front door. I could have died right then and there, but Inez dragged me into a closet and we scrunched down behind a mink coat. I just sat there and stroked it. It was absolutely heavenly."

Lieutenant Rosen looked less than angelic, but he managed a smile. "Do you know who came in downstairs?"

"It was Azalea herself. We heard her talking to that yucky little dog as if he were a baby; it was creepy—to the max. We held our breath for ever and ever, hoping she would leave so that we could get out of there. Just as we had decided to open the bedroom door to see what she was doing, someone else came in. We jumped back into the boudoir and crouched behind the bed. Then we heard voices on the patio, so we slipped down the stairs and ran out the front door."

My stomach flopped like a wrasse on the grass. Caron and Inez had been giggling upstairs—while Mildred was being strangled on the patio. The two could have been found alongside her, with color-coordinated scarves . . . and protruding black tongues.

I found my voice and said, "Why didn't you tell anyone, Caron? You knew that Mildred was killed on the patio below the bedroom window! Weren't you worried that the murderer might have seen you and—"

"Mother, it wasn't the murderer. It was Douglas Twiller." Slowly and patiently, as if I needed precise articulation in order to follow her logic.

"Douglas Twiller?" My mouth fell open. "Are you sure? I thought you heard voices but didn't see anyone?"

Caron shrugged. "Inez peeked out the window."

"But it couldn't have been Douglas," I said slowly, frowning across Caron at Lieutenant Rosen. "He was in my office until three-thirty, then on the other side of the campus with his newest girlfriend. How did he get home and back without being seen?"

He had the courtesy to look equally mystified. "I don't know. There is another little problem, too. If he killed his wife, then who . . . ?"

"Oh, he didn't strangle his wife," Caron chimed in blithely. "He just brought her a tea tray and left. Inez couldn't hear what they said, but she didn't think either of them looked mad. He was kissing her good-bye when we left and saying something about seeing her later, after the reception was over."

We both gaped at her. I said, "I thought Inez took a quick peek and then you two ran down the stairs and left? Were you listening to the conversation as well?"

"I told you we couldn't hear anything, Mother." Indignation coated her voice like an oil slick. "Is that all? I have a midterm paper due Friday, and I'd like to go by the library and pick up a book. Rhonda probably thinks I'm on the bus to Alcatraz by now; I'd like to let her know that I haven't been electrocuted for a simple little prank."

Lieutenant Rosen went over to a vending machine and checked the coin return, carefully avoiding my beady stare. "Just one more thing, Miss Malloy. Did you or Miss Brandon happen to notice a medallion?"

"We saw it in a velvet-lined box on the dresser. I thought it was dumb, but Inez gurgled about it forever. It was silver, with a curly rose on it. Big deal."

"Did you—ah, borrow it?" he said carefully, no doubt mentally reaching for his handcuffs. Petite size.

"I am not a thief!" Caron gave me a startled look. "You know I wouldn't steal anything."

I sighed. "Except for the book on my desk?"

"Books don't count. Besides, it was yours, Mother. You

didn't accuse me of being a thief when I borrowed your hot rollers."

The terminology had come to mind, since they hadn't reappeared in my bedroom for over a week. Nor had my eye shadow. It still hadn't turned up, for that matter.

Lieutenant Rosen interrupted what might have digressed into a family argument, saying, "No one has accused you of being a thief, Miss Malloy. Sometimes a sudden impulse overpowers common sense, that's all. Could Miss Brandon have pocketed the medallion?"

"If she did, I didn't see her do it. What's the big deal anyway? She would have replaced it the next time we were there," Caron muttered, her eyes intent on her sneakers.

"The next time you broke into the house?" I inserted acidly. Fourteen years with the child, and I still found her inscrutable.

"We didn't break anything. We opened the front door and walked in, Mother. If people can't bother to lock their doors, they should accept the fact that other people will come in. It's practically an invitation."

"Lock her up," I told the lieutenant. "There must be some charge that will keep her occupied until college. She can learn the art of basketry in the interim, or how to make license plates."

"Mother!" The lower lip almost bumped the far wall.

"It was only a thought," I snapped. I sent Caron home with an obliging police officer and told her to wait for me. As she slunk out, I heard a muttered threat about her academic record being jeopardized by my insensitivity. It did not merit a response. When she was gone, I said, "Where's the other juvenile delinquent?"

He left for a minute and returned with a worried look.

"They couldn't find her. I don't understand any of this, but I think Miss Brandon's commentary would be valuable."

"It doesn't make any sense. If Douglas strangled Mildred, then who strangled him? I can't believe some enraged romance reader would do the dirty deed, but nobody had any motive. You and I are the only ones who know that he wrote those awful books, including *Professor of Passion*."

"So we are." He put a coin in the machine, pushed a button, and opened a plastic door in the middle of the machine. Coke rained on his hand. He stared at it. "Shit."

I gulped back a semi-hysterical giggle. When he finished wiping his hand on his handkerchief, I said, "Have you checked everyone else's alibis for this afternoon?"

"Jorgeson couldn't find Britton Blake, but he said Maggie Holland was clearing out her desk in Farber Hall. Ms. Holland had nothing much to say about Twiller's death. Very uninterested, Jorgeson said. But, on the other hand, Twiller wasn't popular with either of them." He made a pretense of reading the instructions on the machine. "Where were you, by the way?"

"Are *you* asking *me* for an alibi?" My voice swooped over the pronouns.

"I'm asking you where you were, Mrs. Malloy. Nothing more than that. I'm supposed to ask questions. In fact, I get paid to ask questions."

"Do you think I strangled Mildred and then went after Douglas when I realized my mistake? Do I honestly look like the sort of person who would—who would strangle someone over a stupid book?"

"As you pointed out, you and I are the only ones who know the true identity of Azalea Twilight. No one else had any reason to strangle Twiller."

"How can you accept my hospitality and then accuse me

of murder?" I said hotly as I stood up and started for the door. "You can just solve this yourself, Sherlock. Get your bologna at the grocery store from now on. I don't know who killed the Twillers, and furthermore, I don't care!"

I stomped out of the police station and down the street, the very picture of justifiable outrage. I was at least a mile from the apartment, but I didn't care. The nerve of the man to ask me for an alibi! Oh, he thought he had cause—but the idea was absurd. I slowed down as I swung around the corner and out of sight of the police station. Why would anyone kill Douglas Twiller, except for me? There had to be another motive beyond the libelous material in the book. Which meant I was overlooking someone.

That didn't explain how Douglas had made it home and back without being seen, nor did it explain why he had given Maggie an advance copy of the book—unless he was, as Lieutenant Rosen theorized, trying to manipulate the scene. Douglas hadn't denied it; he had merely refused to elaborate. Perhaps he should have.

I turned on Thurber Street and went to the Book Depot. Locking the door behind me, I wandered between the display shelves to the office. There I found a piece of paper, listed all those involved, drew a few meaningless arrows, and threw the paper in the wastebasket. In novels, the detective is adept at producing a timetable that proves the butler wasn't really in the solarium at half past five. In reality, I had no idea where anyone was at the pertinent times.

That wasn't true, I decided as I fished the paper out again and smoothed it down. Maggie Holland hadn't been at her lawyer's office when Mildred was strangled—and she hadn't been cleaning out her desk when Douglas was murdered. I was at Farber Hall at the time; the building was vacant of anything more substantial than memories. Jorgeson had erred, or the lieutenant had lied to me. The latter seemed more than plausible.

Britton could be on a bus to Kalamazoo, for all I knew. With Inez Brandon, the ringleader and petty thief.

"Shit," I said, echoing an earlier sentiment.

I threw the paper away again, then looked around the office at the piles of clutter, the stacks of unrecorded invoices, the wealth of correspondence from my distributors. I had neglected my store for several days. It seemed like time to retire from the Nancy Drew role and leave the mess in Peter Rosen's lap.

I switched off the light and locked the door, self-discipline having never been one of my strengths. When I arrived at the apartment, I opened Caron's door. She was sprawled across the bed, the telephone receiver embedded in her ear.

Glowering, she said, "What?"

"You read *Professor of Passion*. Was it the copy that was on my desk Sunday afternoon?"

She covered the mouth of the receiver. "I promised I wouldn't read it, Mother, and I didn't."

My little girl scout sounded as if she were facing a tribunal. She seemed to have forgotten our conversation at the kitchen table in the not-too-distant past. Very convenient lapse.

"Then how did you know what was in it?" I countered politely.

"Inez was the one who borrowed it to read. She's only lived in Farberville two or three years; she didn't even catch Dad's name in the plot. She told me every bit of it afterward."

"Where is the copy now?"

"She offered to give it to me after she had finished it, but I didn't want it. We sort of had an argument, and I ended up telling her that Azalea Twilight wrote garbage and that I had thrown my collection away. She was totally offended. Okay, Mother?"

"Are you talking to Inez now?"

"No, Mother, I was talking to Rhonda, but she's probably hung up by now. Or fallen asleep."

"You'll have to risk it," I said. "When you were seen near the Twillers' house, you were staring at something in Inez's hand. If it was the medallion, you'd best tell me."

"It wasn't the medallion, Mother! For that matter, I was too terrified to look at anything, including Inez Brandon's stupid hand. Is that all?"

"Do you have any idea where Inez is?"

"No, and I don't care. She's such an infant that she gets her thrills from reading erotica. It's too immature for words."

I shut the door and went back to the living room, feeling mildly successful. I now knew what had happened to the advance copy. I knew, or hoped I did, the extent of Caron's involvement. She hadn't been an accessory to theft, unless she was lying. She would be in good company if she had. I knew that Maggie had lied, Douglas had lied, and Britton had lied. Mildred Twiller had lived a lie. I had—well, evaded the truth upon occasion, but always with good reason.

It seemed important to locate the medallion. I called Inez's house, but her mother had not seen her since eight that morning and was startled to hear that Inez was not with Caron. It was not the moment to discuss the investigation, or what was separating the girls. We exchanged pleasantries and hung up.

The whole thing had turned into a full-fledged muddle, I decided morosely as I replaced the receiver. Caron and Inez had seen Douglas at his house, at the time he couldn't have been there. He had been kissing his wife on the patio and probably giving her some sort of explanation about the book. Although he had assured me that I would also hear an explanation, he had known that Mildred would be unavailable—in the most permanent way—when the time came. But I didn't believe he had strangled her. There was only one murderer creeping around Farberville. But who?

One pseudo-alibi needed to be exploded. I went down the stairs and knocked on Maggie's door.

"Hello," I said when she appeared. I pushed past her without giving her a chance to remodel my face with the door. "Did you hear that Douglas Twiller was murdered?"

Maggie's face remained blank. "Some cop came by Farber Hall to tell me all about it."

"I was there, but I didn't see you."

"Well, I didn't see you. Does that mean that one of us strangled Douglas Twiller?"

"We'll return to that in a minute, Maggie. First, we're going to discuss Sunday afternoon after the reception. You did not go to your lawyer's office; he was playing golf. Where were you?"

The politically correct posture collapsed. Her shoulders sagged, and her face took on a more human expression. "I did call, but his answering service said they'd have to beep him at the golf course. When I got tired of waiting, I left to warn my lover, a woman in the foreign-language department. We discussed our options the rest of the afternoon. My friend is hoping that she'll be able to stay at Farber, if she can keep her name out of it. None of this is her fault; I've been trying to protect her."

"She's in the foreign-language department?" I repeated, bewildered. I suppose I had presumed that Maggie's friend was the motor-mouthed Sheila Belinski.

"That's right. Do you want her name so that you can lead a witch hunt?" Her cheeks inflated as if she were a blowfish.

"No, Maggie," I said gently. "You said that you were there all afternoon. Did you stay there that evening, too?"

"I decided to find Britton Blake, since he was in the same mess that I was in. I thought we might form an alliance, although it wouldn't have done any good in the long run. Farber College does not allow immoral instructors to teach anything to the innocents—not even poetry. Tuition is too high to risk offending some narrow-minded parent."

"Did you find Britton?"

"He was reeling up Thurber with a troglodyte in white cowboy boots. I could see that we weren't going to engage in meaningful dialogue, since they were cross-eyed and singing at the top of their lungs. I don't think he recognized me."

I found that oddly warming. Britton hadn't been in any condition to strangle Mildred; he couldn't have tied a knot. I checked him off and moved on to the next suspect.

"You weren't at Farber Hall earlier this afternoon," I said. I stopped to think for a minute, then took a chance. "You were with your lover. You must have arrived at Farber Hall after I left and pretended to have been there all afternoon, in order to avoid any names."

"We were saying good-bye," she admitted in a low voice. "I wasn't strangling Douglas Twiller. I yell and scowl a lot, but I don't murder people, Claire."

"I am sorry, Maggie. Your name was dragged through the mud, but not for any good reason. Lieutenant Rosen thinks Douglas was behind the scene from the beginning, that the libel was planned in order to provoke the situation. To give several of us a motive for poor Mildred's death."

She deserved to hear the truth, so I told her about the schizophrenic nature of Azalea Twilight. She wasn't noticeably stunned.

"I suspected as much, but since Twiller had rank, I saw no reason to mention it. So he wrote the trash and she took the credit . . ." Maggie shook her head. "Did he strangle her because she wanted to escape the chauvinistic shackles?"

"No," I sighed. "I won't go into it, but I don't think he did. If nothing else, he wasn't vicious and cold-blooded. He might have devised the whole scheme, but he must have chickened out at the last moment. Someone else finished the scene for him. I wish he had strangled poor Mildred; it would have been tidier."

"Then who did?"

I made a face worthy of Caron's better efforts. "I haven't any idea. Not you, not me, not Britton—who was incapable of knotting his shoelaces. No one else has a motive, unless Stephanie and Derek did it out of an obscure respect for literature."

"Who?" Maggie asked with a nervous gesture, no doubt thinking the mental strain had finally pickled my brain.

"Never mind." I murmured a good-bye and went upstairs to stare out the window at the dark campus across the street. Douglas had manipulated us; that much I accepted. Yet there was still an uncomfortable sense of manipulation by an invisible hand, as though we were puppets. Acts one and two had been played; the third and final act remained. And Douglas was no longer the puppet master.

At last I went to my bedroom and undressed. A mug filled with foul-looking coffee was on the table; I picked it up to study the face of the Professor himself, dear Derek. The moisture from the cup had blurred his features, and his smile was more soggy than arrogant. Stephanie still desired him, however. She glittered at him with an adoration that could not be defrayed by condensation.

I opened the book to the dog-eared page and began to read.

Several hours later I closed the book. It seemed that Stephanie's first love had left her at a Monte Carlo altar in order to smuggle drugs on his yacht. Once on campus, she had nearly been erased by a chicken truck, along with that charmer Martin Carlow, who was. Immediately after the teary memorial service at the campus chapel, Blane Britton had whispered the threat concerning Stephanie's sister. Stephanie failed freshman composition, but her honor remained intact—for the moment.

She sought comfort at the Women's Center. Two pages later, Margaret Holburn tried the thigh gambit. No success. Stephanie's knees were held together by epoxy. Derek was wearing down her resistance by parading around the classroom in tight jeans that emphasized his gender. Stephanie had a difficult time concentrating on Restoration drama.

Just as I thought that my mind would go down with the adverbs, I arrived at the predictably happy ending. The drug runner sank, and the unscrupulous faculty members were exposed. Derek produced the proper solvent, Stephanie's knees sprung open, and they spent at least twenty-five pages on an undulating water bed. Undulating. I survived a bout of sea sickness, but only with a major effort.

Stephanie O'Hara and Derek Dark. A union contrived in heaven and consummated at sea.

Douglas must have modeled Derek on himself, I decided. He was the most ardent believer in his own virility, and the tight jeans would have appealed to his inflated ego. But who had inspired Stephanie? I picked up the book and studied the cover, wondering if there might be a resemblance to someone I knew. If there was, I didn't see it.

The parallels were impossible to miss, yet I was missing the most vital one. Derek was infatuated with the girl. Perhaps she was one of Douglas's notorious coeds. I needed to check the most current list.

I went into the living room and called the police station. I was told that Lieutenant Rosen was at home; did I want his number? I considered mentioning that I had his number—in the metaphorical sense—but amended it to a meek acquiescence.

I dialed the first six digits, faltered, and hung up. I didn't want to wake up his wife or their children, I told myself as I retreated to the kitchen to make tea. I then told myself that I was behaving like an adolescent, turned off the burner, and went back to the telephone. To hell with his wife, I added sweetly. Let her worry about calls from women in the middle of the night. He could use his limited wits to pacify her; it was not my problem.

Sherlock answered on the twelfth ring. "Yeah?"

"Did I wake you up?" I said, very polite.

"No, that's all right. I fell asleep in front of the television. Do you know who won the football game?"

"This is a bit more important than twenty grown men jumping on each other to capture a porcine ball," I said, less polite.

"Twenty-two."

I gave the receiver a puzzled frown. "What are you talking about? Are you sure you're awake?"

After a pause, he said, "Each football team has eleven players. Eleven times two is twenty-two."

"I have no interest in football, Lieutenant Rosen, nor in simple arithmetic functions. Don't you think you ought to be more concerned about the identity of the person who murdered the Twillers?"

This time the pause lasted a full minute. Finally, sounding more awake, he said, "Do you know who it is?"

"No. Do you?"

"I don't even know who won the Houston game," he growled.

"Are we back to that? If you prefer to discuss games, wake up your wife. I'll wait until you've worked it out of your system, and then we can move onto more important things."

He hung up, which I found more than a little rude. I hadn't had a chance to ask him if Douglas had carried on with some coed named Stephanie . . . or with a name that might be twisted to Stephanie. I needed to discover the names of Douglas Twiller's last few conquests, from the secretary through the latest who had given him an alibi.

I climbed in bed and pulled the pillow over my head. Although I tried to concentrate on the characters in the book, my mind found a diversion that was irrelevant, trivial, and totally pointless: Did I wake up the insufferable man's wife, and did I care?

ELEVEN

I opened the Book Depot as usual the next day and put in several hours of labor on the paperwork. When my accountant called, I was able to tell him that I would drop off the ledger that afternoon. It was a bluff, a familiar one. He laughed, I laughed, and we hung up amid the glee.

The Farberville CID kept a civilized distance. During one of many lulls, I took a sports encyclopedia off the rack to see if football was indeed played by eleven neckless hunks, rather than ten, which would be an easier number to remember. Eleven. I wondered if the lieutenant had taken a lucky guess or whether it was public knowledge. Why eleven? Twelve would have made more sense—an even dozen. Azalea had written thirteen, a baker's dozen and not a propitious number for either Twiller.

Late in the morning Caron called. After a rushed promise that she was between classes rather than skipping one, she told me that Inez had not shown up for school. She sounded worried, as though she had forgotten all the snide comments she had been making since the spat began. I told her to go to class, and I unconsciously began to straighten books on the display shelves. All the copies of *Professor of Passion* were still there; not even the substantial, gruesome accounts in the newspaper were enough to move them.

Flattening Derek's dimple with my thumb, I squinted at the image of Stephanie, determined to find some hint. Nothing. She had a lovely face, if one preferred a total lack of character coupled with a certain dimness. An intellectual midget, but a passionate one.

My aged hippie shambled in to see if I had received any new science-fiction epics. I greeted him absently, already back to the ledger. I looked up when he made a rumbling noise. He was in front of the display where Derek and Stephanie sat three-deep, waiting to be banished to the paperback graveyard.

"That's the book!" he chortled, jabbing his finger at it.

"That's a book," I corrected him with a trace of tartness. "In that this is a bookstore, there are many of them. The sci-fi is on the second row."

He gave me a wondering look. "I read this, you know."

"So did I, and it wasn't very good."

"But it was interesting," he said under his breath. He looked as though he might be considering buying all the copies for some obscure reason. The idea was obscene: Derek and Stephanie in every corner, on every table, on every bookshelf.

"Why was it interesting?" I said, coldly prepared to explode whatever myth he had about the book and get him back to the science-fiction rack.

He scratched his beard. "Well, that woman was quite a bitch. All the men kept after her, but I wouldn't have trusted her as far as I could throw a laser eradicator. And the things they did in bed . . . can people really do that?"

"If they have worked in a circus. Which woman?"

He put his finger on Stephanie's limpid face. "Her."

I took the man's arm and led him to a new arrival that featured giant armadillos in battle with a gelatinous clump of brain cells for supremacy over a sandy asteroid.

"This is on me," I said, gave him the book, and shoved him out the door of the Book Depot as graciously as possible.

Stephanie quite a bitch? I shook my head. Stephanie was a sweet, simple-minded soul who was forever having to resist amorous advances. Douglas knew the rules of the genre; he wouldn't have added anything that would risk the necessity of revisions. He had known precisely how much he earned for each hour at the typewriter. He would not have written something that might water down the figure. Not consciously, anyway.

I went home for a sandwich and a cup of tea. An envelope was taped on the door, the handwriting familiar. I carried it to the kitchen table and sat down to read it.

> Dear Claire,
>
> "The ability to make love frivolously is the chief characteristic which distinguishes human beings from the beast." Heywood Campbell Broun, 1888–1939. It seems I failed to make the distinction. Despite appearances, frivolity was never my forte. The little girl lied about her age, among other things, but it was clearly my fault. "Leave-takings are but wasted sadness. Let me pass out quietly." Jerome Jerome, 1859–1927.
>
> Britton

Well done. I gave him a few seconds of mental applause, then folded the note and put it in the drawer beside my bed. I was relieved that he had chosen to say good-bye in a note;

I wouldn't have had enough self-control to see him in person. The little girl and Caron were approximately the same age, for God's sake. Puberty is hard, if not impossible, to hide. Or had Britton believed the girl was all of sixteen or seventeen?

The girl. Her abortion and death were now publicized nationwide, courtesy of paperback racks in every place from grocery stores to gas stations. Could someone have recognized the character and murdered Mildred out of some distorted sense of vengeance? Or, I added slowly, had the someone in question used Azalea's book to destroy Britton? A team effort, in which each conspirator was allowed to pick a victim.

At this point, I did something for which I shall always carry a gram or two of guilt. I searched Caron's room, from the dustiest corner under the bed to the crumb-infested top shelf in her closet. I was fairly sure she didn't have a silver medallion stashed somewhere, but I wanted to be certain. In the delivery room, mothers are given a few privileges in exchange for the unpleasantness; one is the inalienable right to pry.

While I was teetering on a chair to reach the back corner of the top shelf, the downstairs doorbell buzzed. Grumbling, I went to the living room window and looked down at the porch. The crown of black curls below belonged to none other than Lieutenant Rosen. I glanced at a nearby vase, certainly heavy enough to be lethal. Tut, tut.

I went downstairs to let him in. "No paddy wagon?"

"Farberville doesn't have a paddy wagon. It's on the list, after the thumb screws." He smiled sweetly. "Is Miss Brandon here, by any chance? She seems to have misplaced herself since yesterday afternoon, and her mother is worried, as is the principal at the school."

"Why would she be here? Caron's at school." I mirrored his smile and tried to close the door. "Your foot, Lieutenant—it's in the way."

"So it is." He brushed past me, went upstairs, and waited on the landing for me to join him. "Coffee sounds good."

"Are you here to arrest me or to suggest a kaffeklatsch?"

"Well," he said as we went into the living room, "I haven't decided whom to arrest yet, but your name is on the list. However, there's no big rush. Tell me where everything is and I'll start the coffee. You ought to sit down; you're pale."

It was too insane to handle. I sat down, meekly told him where the coffee was, and listened to him putter around my kitchen. My name was on the list. Was Caron's? While I worried, he puttered through the whole apartment and back to the living room.

"Miss Brandon isn't here," he informed me cheerfully.

"Brilliant deduction, Sherlock. Did you look in all the closets and drawers, in case I chopped her up and put her in Baggies?" Not funny, but I was tired of his arrogance. Rosen and Derek. That brought me back to a question that hadn't been answered. "Did you ever find out whom Douglas Twiller was—er, seeing when Mildred was strangled?"

"I wish you'd stay out of this, Mrs. Malloy."

"Why do you insist on dragging me in?"

He pursed his lips. "I don't know. If you'd like to get out of the game, you could simply stop hiding things from me and tell me what you know. Then you could run a bookstore and I could run an investigation."

I made a pretense of yawning and said, "Is the coffee ready? I'm on the verge of a nap."

He stomped into the kitchen, clattered my dishes with uncalled-for vigor, and reappeared with two mugs of coffee. "Why do you want to know about Twiller's girlfriend? She's not involved."

"What's her name?" I persisted.

He consulted his notebook. "Andrea Piedmont. She transferred to Farber from the University of Florida. She claimed that her affair with Twiller began Sunday afternoon, when he showed up at her apartment. Other than that, she has no knowledge of anything even vaguely relating to the others."

As adept as I am with anagrams, I couldn't get Andrea to Stephanie without stretching—severely. "Who before Andrea?" I asked, sipping the coffee and struggling for nonchalance.

He flipped through the notebook. "No one could suggest a name, although everybody agreed that there must have been someone. We tried to chase down a rumor about a secretary in the English department, but the secretaries clammed up."

"It's someone who transferred out of the English department," I said absently. "But Douglas told me that that affair was over months ago. He hardly ever let a week go by without finding a new victim." Victim was a poor choice of words. There were already too many victims in Farberville for it to ever quite be the same.

As he scribbled in his notebook, he said, "You see, you can tell me things if you try. It didn't hurt too badly."

"Why don't you try a little reciprocity?" I said. "Did you figure out how Douglas made it to his house and back without being seen by either Sheila or me? Caron saw him between three-fifteen and three-twenty, when I was on the railroad tracks and Sheila on Arbor Street above me."

"Twiller insisted that he had not been there, despite Caron's statement to the contrary. To my regret, he was strangled before I could pursue the problem."

"Your regret, Lieutenant Rosen?"

His expression would have wilted a head of lettuce. "I discussed the problem with Miss Belinski only this morning. Around three-twenty, she turned the corner and came in this direction to look for Miss Holland. Twiller must have waited until the sidewalk was empty, then hurried back to the Book Depot. He went in the back, waited until he heard your voice, and then strolled up the aisle from the office."

"How did he get there in the first place?"

"He must have gone straight out the back door and down the railroad tracks. According to your story, you stayed at the reception for a few minutes before you flounced out."

"Strolled out," I corrected him coldly.

"Whatever. He did have time to make it home."

"Why? Why did he lie—when all he had to do was say that he wanted to go home to see how Mildred was? It makes no sense whatever, unless he planned to murder his wife! If he did, then who murdered him? I don't understand!"

Lieutenant Rosen blinked in the face of the hurricane. "I don't understand, Jorgeson doesn't understand, and Mildred Twiller in her grave probably doesn't understand. Why should you?"

Abruptly I was in the eye of the hurricane, where it was ominously calm. The first order of business was to rid myself of the lieutenant. "I'm sorry. You're the detective. After you and Jorgeson are satisfied, you can come to show-and-tell. I've got to go back to the store now; there are a lot of customers early in the afternoon."

I stood up, found my purse, and shooed him downstairs

and out the front door to his car. Although he seemed suspicious, he eventually pulled away from the curb and disappeared around the corner. I held my ground in case he went around the block and came back to see what I was doing—which I wasn't about to share.

Five minutes later I could no longer bear to wait. I hopped in my car and drove toward the cemetery to find Inez. Where else could she be? Not at home or at school, not at my apartment. The child had a very narrow range—and a vivid imagination, coupled with an Azalean obsession. Once Caron betrayed her, she would head straight for a marble block adorned with cupids: Mildred Twiller's grave.

There were no limousines this time, nor any subdued mourners circling the fresh mound of dirt. I peered into the trees as I approached the area, but there was no figure cowering into the shadows as there had been previously.

"Fiddlesticks," I grumbled, deflated by failure. It had been such a wonderful theory, logical and precise, dictated by knowledge of the girl and her mind. She really ought to have been there.

I perused the stone, compelled as always to read the written word, no matter where it was. Mildred had been fifty-seven when she died, I computed with a sigh. And she had *Flown to That Place Where Love Is Eternal*, according to the gothic script below her name. Touching, in a silly way. Mildred would have adored it.

As I bent down to rearrange a vase of chrysanthemums, a flash of light caught my attention. I tossed the cardboard vase aside and pushed back a layer of dried rose petals. The medallion glittered at me from under a clump of dirt.

Dirt, to my knowledge, doesn't take fingerprints. I could have called the police station to report my discovery, I suppose. But Lieutenant Rosen had just searched my apartment to see if I had Inez's body in a suitcase; I wasn't feeling terribly kindly toward him. Also, if Inez had stolen the medallion, then Caron might have lied earlier. I wasn't sure whether or not it was a crime to lie to the police. I was sure, on the other hand, that it was not a particularly good idea to incense the lieutenant. I knew that much from personal experience.

I picked up the medallion and put it in my pocket. I looked about once more for Inez, now convinced that she was nearby. A figure shuffled into view on the far side of the cemetery, a bulky man in a dark blue navy surplus jacket and a knitted cap. He was raking leaves from between the rows of white marble teeth, as though he were some sort of macabre dental hygienist.

"Hey there," I called as I approached him.

He gave me a leery look but stopped raking and waited. His eyes were pink and watery, his mouth slightly agape. Except for his face, every bit of exposed flesh was covered with thick black hair. Not the most astute source of information. I decided, but capable of a grunted response—which he made.

"Did you see a teenage girl over that way?" I asked.

"Over what way, lady?" He leaned on the handle of the rake and smacked his lips.

"By the new grave. There, on the hillside just this side of the dogwood trees."

"Dogwood trees? I don't know nothing about trees, lady. Except they have a lot of leaves that have to be raked up and burnt." The smacking accelerated.

"Where's your supervisor?" I demanded.

"He'll be back at five o'clock to pay me for raking the

leaves. He'll dock me if I don't get done. Costs me money to talk, lady."

Message received. I took the lone five-dollar bill out of my purse and waved it under his nose. "Did you see anyone in the cemetery this afternoon?"

He reached for the bill, but I retreated and tightened my grip. I repeated the question.

"Yeah," he said, "there was a girl over there by them dogwood trees when I got here. Sitting by a grave, moaning and rocking."

We repeated the dance. He reached; I retreated. I let it flutter temptingly for a second, then said, "What did she look like?"

"A girl." He shrugged and stared ravenously at the bill. I could almost feel his wet lips on my fingers. Yuck to the max.

"How long ago did she leave?"

He gave me an indignant look. "I was raking leaves, lady. I don't make enough money to buy fancy watches on minimum wage. I can barely afford wine with dinner."

Wine *was* dinner, I thought with a grim smile. I doubted I would hear anything more enlightening, so I handed him the five and turned to leave. Dark, smoky clouds had rolled in since the morning, and now a sudden gust of wind caught the man's pile of leaves and sent them tumbling away. Behind the distant mountains, thunder rumbled.

I left the man to chase his leaves, hoping that it would take at least five dollars worth of added energy. My fingers curled around the medallion in my pocket, I angled past Mildred's grave for a final glance, then went to my car before the rain could catch me.

I sat there for a long time. Where in God's name was Inez? She had been at the cemetery and, from the guttural description, had been more than a little miserable. Who wouldn't be—sitting on a fresh grave under a dull gray sky?

She had, apparently, returned the medallion in a typically Inez fashion. No doubt she had recited some of her favorite passages and scattered rose petals for effect. But now where had she gone? A tap on the window almost gave me a heart attack.

"Lady," my simian snitch yelled, gesturing at me to roll down the window. He held the rake like a scepter, the emperor of autumn. His fingers were all thicker than my big toe.

"Yes?" I managed to say.

"There was someone else."

"Someone else?" I goggled at him. "Who?"

He rubbed his fingers together in an age-old sign that implied a necessary exchange, money being my contribution. I looked in my wallet. It was empty, except for a glueless postage stamp and Caron's library card. In the bottom of my purse I found a few pennies, dimes, and nickles. I dug them out.

"Is this enough?"

His lips moved as he counted the meager collection of coins. When he arrived at a total, he gave me a wounded stare. "Eighty-nine cents? You've got to be kidding, lady. I wouldn't tell you your mother's name for eighty-nine cents."

"You don't know my mother's name. Besides, it is possible there is a cold-blooded killer after that girl."

"It was more likely your mother." He turned around to stalk off, his massive shoulders hunched with anger. I couldn't blame him; eighty-nine cents is not exactly an IRA for old age.

"Wait," I howled in desperation, "will you take a check?"

He stopped to consider, while I glared at his back with all the venom I could muster. At last he turned around slowly to study first my battered car and then my distorted expression. "How do I know your check is any good?"

"It's better than nothing," I retorted. When he shook his head, I decided to risk it all with a grandiose gesture. I switched on the engine and let the car roll a few inches. "A twenty-dollar check," I called in farewell.

"You have identification?" He was moving toward me like a carnivorous dinosaur advancing on a vegetarian sibling.

"A driver's license and two credit cards," I countered. "You'll have to settle for that, unless you take MasterCard, buddy."

"Yeah, I suppose I'll take a check," he conceded. "Leave the name off; I'll write it in myself. I don't want no trouble from my supervisor."

He waited until I had written the check, then peered suspiciously at the name and address in the corner, perhaps expecting to see the name of a mental hospital. Fighting back an urge to rip whatever he knew from between his ears, I fumed until he seemed satisfied.

When the check disappeared, I said, "Well? Who else was here with the girl?"

"Another girl." He found that highly amusing, if the gurgled snorts were to be interpreted as laughter. His shoulders started to heave; his eyes disappeared into folds of flesh; his mouth could have sheltered a hibernating bear. The noise sent a flock of sparrows into a treetop.

I tried to convince myself that he hadn't meant Caron. The world was populated by millions of girls, from the pigtail variety to those with sequined glasses and henna rinses. Farber College enrolled three thousand of them every year. The public schools were rife with them. Caron had called from school, and that was where she was. She could not have come to the cemetery. I was being hysterical, to put it mildly.

Quasimodo finally ceased the gurgles and started to walk away. "Come back here," I said in the voice that stops even Caron. "For twenty dollars, I think I deserve more than two words."

"Hey, lady, it was some girl in a raincoat and a scarf. She had a regular face, arms and legs, all the normal stuff. She sat down next to the first one and they had a long talk, then they got up and left together. They did not come over to where I was raking to tell me where they were going."

"What color was her hair?"

"Blue."

I wondered if I had anything in my glove compartment that might serve as a weapon. "Blue?" I repeated, raising my eyebrows.

"She had on a scarf, lady. All I saw was blue." Again, he started to lumber off, my check clutched in his paws.

"The information wasn't worth eighty-nine cents," I said to his back.

"Raking ain't worth minimum wage. Life's tough, lady."

At this point, I was furious enough to leap on his back and cling with grim determination until he told me the entire story. I had opened the door when another car pulled in behind mine. Guess who? Lieutenant Rosen climbed out, waved to me, and walked up to the gorilla.

"Well, Hendrix?" he murmured.

I scrambled out of my car and stomped across the gravel. "Hendrix? Hendrix?" I screeched.

Lieutenant Rosen smiled. "Mrs. Malloy, this is Corporal Hendrix, one of our plainclothes officers. Corporal Hendrix, Mrs. Malloy. Now, if you'll excuse us, Mrs. Malloy, I'd like to hear the report . . ."

"He's a cop?" I was still screeching, despite the social niceties. "Is he allowed to take bribes from innocent citizens? He has twenty-five dollars of my money. In payola, or blackmail or something! I want him arrested right now!"

"Let me hear his report first, and then we'll discuss financial matters." He took the man's arm and tried to escape. Hendrix gave me a look that was, no doubt, supposed to suffice as an apology. It did not come close.

I raised my voice to its maximum volume. "You come back here! I want to hear the report, too, or I'll—I'll call the FBI and tell them about the bribe! I cannot believe that you permit this swamp creature to lie to citizens who are merely trying to—"

"Yes?" Sherlock said encouragingly. "Trying to—?"

Well, there wasn't a clever way to finish the sentence; we both knew that. I decided on a new ploy. "Please, I'd like to know if my daughter was in the cemetery with Inez Brandon." Miss Manners would have been proud of me.

When Rosen nodded, Hendrix said, "I couldn't see the second girl well enough to determine any identifying factors. Sorry. When I moved closer, they left."

"But the first girl was Miss Brandon?" Supercop asked.

Hendrix looked at the distant grave. "I'm fairly sure that it was Miss Brandon. Brown hair, glasses, slender, and sort of—"

"Cowering?" I suggested.

He seemed pleased to find the perfect word. "Cowering, that's right. Can I go back to the station, Lieutenant? I think

I'm getting a blister." He held up a paw to show us, noticed the check, and handed it to me with an embarrassed look.

"Why were you so impossible?" I said coldly.

"Orders, ma'am."

After he was gone, I stared at Lieutenant Rosen. "Orders?"

"Indeed, Mrs. Malloy." He turned on the smile, but his eyes contradicted the warmth. "You have a nasty habit of showing up wherever you're not wanted. I realize that you're worried about your daughter, but this is a murder investigation—and I'm in charge. You're likely to end up with a scarf around your neck, too."

So he had the nerve to think I was the one who was interfering! I snorted disdainfully and spun on my heel to leave. "A pity, Lieutenant Rosen. And just when I was prepared to tell you where Inez is at this moment and with whom. But if you don't care to listen to my theories, then I'll go back to my little store to peddle my little books. Good-bye!"

He should have stopped me. He should have apologized for the insulting remarks and begged me to share my insights. He should have fallen to his knees and pleaded with me.

"Good-bye," he said.

TWELVE

Caron was hovering at the door when I arrived home. She grabbed my arm before I could take off my coat. "Did you find Inez? Her mother came by the school, and then some policeman had me paged to the office to ask if I knew where she was. I couldn't tell them anything, Mother. I haven't seen Inez in days and days and days." She seemed to feel she was describing centuries at the very least.

I disengaged my arm to put down my purse. "I just came from the cemetery, where I found this." I took the medallion out of my pocket to show it to her. "Inez left it on poor Mildred's grave, as some sort of gesture. I don't know where she is right now, but at least I know where she's been in the last few hours."

"She was at the cemetery?" Caron yelped. "Creepy."

"Earlier this afternoon," I said. "Apparently she sat next to Mildred Twiller's grave and did a mourning routine. Then she hid the medallion under a sprinkle of rose petals."

"Inez is flipped out about Azalea. She was totally offended when I trashed my collection. You would have thought I had thrown away some old saint's bones or something."

"Did she take my autographed copy of *Professor of Passion*, along with the copy on my desk?"

Caron's head bobbled like that of a deboned hen. "Yours, and about twelve others. When we were cleaning up the Book Depot, we found a bunch of copies hidden in funny places. There were three behind the toilet and one stuck in the fern. Four more were in the nonfiction rack. Inez thought she was in heaven, for Pete's sake!"

"So she did take the medallion," I said to myself, imagining the girl pining over her pitiful booty.

Caron's head switched from vertical to horizontal bobbles. "I've been trying to remember exactly what happened, and I don't think she did. I think I saw it in the box just as we went out the bedroom door, and she didn't go back later. She was with me the rest of the afternoon at the Book Depot and then at the library."

"So she didn't take the medallion," I mused, frowning. Then the other girl at the cemetery had brought it and allowed Inez to bury it under the rose petals. They had left minutes later, when Hendrix—the vile gorilla—tried to creep near them.

I made a pot of tea and sat down at the kitchen table to think. Despite my show of bravado at the cemetery, I only suspected I knew where Inez was. The other girl—thank God, not Caron—had to be one of Douglas Twiller's objects of passion, the one who became Stephanie in his final opus. The invisible character. The one my hippie had described as "quite a bitch."

But I had been concerned about Douglas's most recent

slate of women, which I suddenly realized was irrelevant. *Professor of Passion* had been written at least nine months ago. Submission, editing, minor revisions, and then a period of time to be published—the book was a historical rather than a current-events exposé.

No one, not even Hercule Poirot himself, can easily recite the months backward. I found a calendar in a drawer and flipped back ten months. January, give or take a month. How on earth could I find out whom Douglas was tutoring in bedroom techniques that long ago? Perplexed, I sat and idly read all the scribbled notations on the calendar while I tried to think of my next move.

January had been a lean social month. Britton's name appeared in a few places, along with times for cocktail parties and dinner dates. We hadn't attended anything of importance, except for a few college functions and the inescapable gallery openings, mandatory for the faculty whenever a new set of paintings or sculptures is moved in. During the month, the Twillers had not invited us over one time to meet Douglas's current paramour.

"I guess I'll have to go and see for myself," I said under my breath. I drank the last of my tea, put on my coat, and went to the door of Caron's bedroom. "I'm going out for a few minutes. If anyone calls, take a message."

She lowered a copy of *Wuthering Heights*. "Are you going to find Inez?" she asked in a thin voice.

"Probably not, but I'm going to try."

On that dismal note, I left the apartment and walked down the hill toward Arbor Street and the railroad tracks. I turned left at the bridge, passed the second bridge, and ultimately stopped in front of the Twiller house.

It rose behind the fence like a black monolith. I assumed that Camille had scuttled away to different lodgings once the police had finished with her; considering the proliferation of bodies in the house, I should have done the same. The window on the second floor of the carriage house was dark. The gardener, too, had gone. Twilliam had no doubt been incarcerated at the pound, or whatever is done with orphaned dogs.

I opened the gate and went up the sidewalk to the porch, feeling increasingly silly. I had expended most of my courage to get this far; Inez was nearly twenty-five years younger than I and a good deal more timid. My theory of Inez's whereabouts was turning to lace—full of holes. But, I scolded myself, I certainly could check to make sure the house was empty before I slithered away like the craven coward I was.

The front door was locked. I went down the steps and around to the side yard, squinting at the black holes that were, in previous days, windows covered with delicate, fluttering sheers. No ghastly white face looked back at me. I would have instinctively dived down a snake hole had that happened. I hate snakes, but I hate ghastly white faces more.

I continued to the backyard. The furniture on the patio had been put away; the concrete surface glistened like an ice rink. I cupped my hands on the glass door to peer into the living room. There, the furniture was already shrouded. A poor choice of words.

Eventually, I made my way completely around the house, still very much on the outside. By this time, I did not believe there was anyone on the inside, but I had regained a bit of courage. Tapping my foot, I glanced around for the most likely place to hide the spare house key. We still do that in Farberville, despite the national trend to the contrary.

After all, one does get locked out on occasion. The trick was to fool the potential burglars without tricking oneself.

I fumbled around in the dark, checking various rocks and flowerpots. I found the key under a pot of shriveled geraniums. Mildred wasn't terribly imaginative; my own key is taped under an eave on the porch. Don't mention that to swarthy men in pseudo-leather jackets, please.

The discovery left an ambivalent taste. I finally persuaded myself to unlock the door and tiptoe into the foyer. The den was on the right, I remembered, and the living room on the left. The stairs were visible in the faint glow from the streetlight, wide and inviting. Nancy Drew would have dashed right up them. I went into the living room to look around.

"Inez?" I whispered. I dodged a table and went to the kitchen. The counters were bare; the refrigerator silenced by the removal of its lifeline. No one sat at the dining room table to greet me. In that I would have had a stroke, I was not dismayed.

The ground floor was vacant. That left the upstairs—the white boudoir that wasn't mauve and pink. "Okay, Nancy Drew," I muttered, biting my lip unmercifully, "let's take a look."

I managed to produce a few murmured *Inez?*'s as I crept up the stairs. I did not hear a faint *Yes?* whispered in response. I didn't hear anything, and I didn't care for the situation one bit. I despise books in which the heroine strolls into danger, humming the national anthem and not bothering to sweat. Totally unrealistic, I told myself as I wiped the copious sweat out of my eyes. I don't even like brave spies. I prefer sensible people who wait for the police. Why wasn't I at the nearest pay phone?

All this drifted around inside my head as I reached the

second floor. I wasn't feeling particularly brave, but, to be frank, I wasn't planning to meet any monsters—or murderers—on the landing. I had reached the stage of feeling downright silly as I murmured a final, "Inez?"

"Mrs. Malloy?" Softly, frightened.

I grabbed the banister. "Inez?" I managed to croak without keeling over on the shag carpet.

"Mrs. Malloy?"

We were not making admirable progress. Rather than respond once again with her name, I opted to find the source of the panicked answer. I sidled down the hallway to the last door, eased it open, and said, "Inez?"

No luck. I retraced my path, peering into the dim interiors for a sign of life. I found a closet with folded linens, a bathroom, a guest room, and finally the boudoir. It resembled the internal cavity of a great white whale. For the umpteenth time I hissed, "Inez?"

"Mrs. Malloy?"

"This is not blind man's bluff," I snapped testily. "If you're in here, I'd appreciate a signal. I'm tired of trailing a leaky tire."

She gulped wetly and said, "Mrs. Malloy, I'm in here. I'm sorry that I can't get up to say hello."

Inez would probably apologize for labor pains, if she lived that long. I stumbled into the room until my shin found a chair. "Are you on the bed?"

"Yes, ma'am. I'm sort of tied up."

"Sort of tied up, Inez? That's similar to sort of pregnant or sort of dead. You either are or you aren't." It wasn't terribly sympathetic, but it was terribly realistic. The cowering girl was responsible for a great deal of embarrassment, beginning with the police station and ending in the cemetery with Officer Hendrix. It wasn't totally her fault. Not more than ninety-five percent, anyway.

"Very tied up," she murmured from the darkness that had assailed my shin. "Ropes, and a belt."

"Perhaps I should untie you?" I started toward the disembodied voice, my hands held in front of me.

A voice from behind me stopped me in midstep. "Ah, Mrs. Malloy, you've finally joined us. How lovely; I was hoping you might come."

Lieutenant Rosen's voice would have been welcome, despite my incessant gripes. On the contrary, Sheila Belinski's voice sent a shiver down my spine, as though she'd drawn an icicle along it.

"Sheila," I said, "what are you doing here?"

Inez whimpered, but I thought it prudent to leave her where she was. I turned around to peer into the blackness to locate the slender figure with murderous intent.

"The girl and I came here to make sure that someone had taken care of Twilliam," Sheila said. "We're the only two that care about Azalea Twilight, aren't we, Inez? Azalea loved little Twilliam, and we were very worried about him." Her voice had the sibilant quality of a three-year-old, but the sarcasm was ripe with age.

Inez wasn't any Einstein, but she knew enough to mumble, "That's right, Mrs. Malloy, we came to see if someone had taken care of Azalea's puppy."

"And when you didn't find Twilliam, you decided to tie yourself up on the bed?" I said calmly. Silent night, holy night, all is calm, all is bright.

"Inez is very observant," Sheila snickered from the impenetrable shadows. "She asked me precisely when I had picked up the stupid medallion. It seems she had toyed with it just before Mildred was murdered, and she couldn't understand why I had it. Inez inquired so nicely that I told her."

She took a deep breath, as if to crow. And crow she did, although with modest restraint. "I picked it up after I strangled Mrs. Twiller, naturally, but I didn't want to tell Inez that until she was properly positioned. I just let her play her melodramatic game at the cemetery, then brought her here to wait for you. I knew you'd come."

It was time for a demonstration of my innate authoritativeness. "And why was that, Sheila?" I demanded in a stern tone.

"Because I wanted you here," she said smugly.

I didn't like that at all. The damned woman was implying that I was a marionette on a conveniently long string. She held the end. Twitch, twitch; hello, Mrs. Malloy.

"Congratulations, Sheila, I am indeed here. Now that you've shown your cunningness, why don't we turn on a light so that I can untie Inez?"

"Because I don't want to," she said. An audible gloat drifted out of the darkness. "The switch is behind me, Mrs. Mallory; I doubt that you could find it in time."

"Why involve me in all this?" I asked.

"Oh, you're very much a part of my play. In fact, you'll have the starring role in the final scene!"

I shrank from the voice. "I fail to see how Inez is involved, Sheila. After all, she didn't really see anything. She only appeared in the wrong places at the wrong times."

As Nancy Drew, I was supposed to distract the deranged killer until the police burst through the door, brandishing guns and shouting Miranda cautions. The major flaw in my plot was that the police, unless they were clairvoyant, were probably drinking sodas in their plastic lounge. Poor planning on my part. I sent a word of apology to Lieutenant

Rosen—in case he was listening. His record to date was not good.

Sheila seemed to read my less-than-encouraging thoughts. "No one knows that we're here, Mrs. Malloy. Once I take care of you and the girl, I'll go back to my dorm room and pack my bags. No one will even notice that I'm missing."

"Get off it, Sheila!" I snapped. "You're forever claiming that no one notices you. I noticed you, for God's sake. And"—I stopped to take a breath—"Douglas Twiller noticed you, too. About a year ago, I would guess?"

"We loved each other. When we first met, our hearts cried out as if they were a single voice. He treasured me, called me his precious flower."

Inez was grunting and groaning, but not in pain. Azalean fantasies were shallow nursery tales compared to the real-life romance taking form in the inky boudoir. She loved it; I could hear her eyelashes fluttering.

Before she could contribute any snippets of kindling, I said, "You also had a more prosaic relationship with Douglas Twiller, didn't you? The typical affair, bed included amid the poetic avowals?"

Sheila made a noise not unlike the noises coming from the bed. "It was more than an affair, Mrs. Malloy. Douglas loved me, and he wanted to spend his life with me. He was caught in his wife's vicious snares, however. It was all that stood between us and happiness."

"Mildred's snares?" I laughed crudely. "Mildred Twiller couldn't snare a handicapped hamster. If Douglas told you that, then he was lying. He was worried about the chairmanship of the English department—they prefer Puritans to satyrs."

Sheila's voice seemed closer as she said, "I finally

realized that, Mrs. Malloy. When you told me that he was with another woman, I decided that he was no longer worth the threat he imposed. I took care of him, too."

Behind me Inez was positively percolating, which wasn't going to help. Swatting at her with my hand, I said, "But why did you kill Mildred Twiller? Divorce court would have been easier."

"Douglas swore that a divorce would destroy her. I tried to point out that that was the idea, but he was too soft-hearted," Sheila hissed, closer. "We were in love, Mrs. Malloy. Not the tawdry sort of love he described in trashy books; it was a pure, unsullied love. There was never any physical anxiety; we wanted only the spiritual bonds to bring us together."

That and the Easter Bunny, I told myself. The affair with Sheila must have been a classic in manly deception. It began a year or so ago, I added with a flicker of insight, after a gallery opening. Sheila, thrilled over her pots; Douglas, properly flattering. A hushed conversation in a corner of the gallery, a request to visit her studio, eyes meeting over the rims of plastic champagne glasses. One thing, without fail, had tumbled into another. But Douglas hadn't made quite the commitment Sheila had.

I decided that I was obliged to keep her talking, so that the CID could have time to slither up the stairs. Again, a nagging problem. No CID. I took a deep breath and said, "Then why did you kill Douglas, Sheila? Surely your love could have risen above the latest cheap affair. If he was such a great lover—?"

"He was a coward!" she snapped. "I showed him how to get rid of his wife. We put everyone in the stupid book, so that all of you would have a motive to kill her. I told him everything he needed. All he had to do was tie the knot and get back to the scuzzy bookstore before anyone noticed he wasn't in the office. But, nooooooo, he chickened out. He couldn't do it—so I did!"

"Did he tell you he couldn't go though with it when he met you on the sidewalk?" I leaned back to fumble for Inez's binding. Inez wasn't going to be much help, but there wasn't a Mountie within a thousand miles. Inez Brandon and Claire Malloy take on King Kong—a late-night classic. A classic disaster.

"The wimp!" she said scornfully. From the near shadows. Much too close. Much too sibilant.

"So you went on to the house, tidied up for him, then swore you hadn't seen him," I suggested, clawing at the knot around Inez's ankles.

"That's correct, Mrs. Malloy. After all the planning, I couldn't let all those motives fade away. It worked beautifully; you, Britton Blake, and Maggie were all furious enough to strangle Mrs. Twiller. What a shame the detective couldn't pin it on any of you. I did try to drop a few hints, but he couldn't follow any of them.

"A shame," I agreed. The rope was loosened, but I couldn't find the belt buckle that kept Inez's hands behind her back. Once free, I prayed the two of us could do something worthy of the sisterhood—a tackle to the midriff, hair-pulling, whatever.

"I have a gun," Sheila said in a conversational voice. I opted to forget the physical ploys. Something subtle.

"So what?" I said, laughing as if my life depended on it.

"I'm afraid I have few options, Mrs. Malloy. If I don't shoot you and Inez, then you'll tell tales to that horrid detective. If I do, then—why, no one will suspect me. After all, I wrote the final scene for you and you alone. Inez is simply an extra who should have stayed in the wings."

I unbuckled Inez and finally found the last knot on her ankles. Since I couldn't give her any advice without being shot, I squeezed her shoulder and straightened up. "It won't work, Sheila. I found the medallion at the cemetery and gave it to Lieutenant Rosen. He'll be here in a matter of minutes."

"He knows we're in the Twiller house?" She chuckled merrily, albeit with a brittle edge. "How quaint, Mrs. Malloy. He doesn't know we're here. The house is dark, the door locked. No one knows we're here—except for us. In the immediate future, there'll be only one of us to know even that much."

She wasn't including Inez or me in the count. One—and two dead bodies. I shoved Inez hard enough to roll her off the far side of the bed. Then I said, "The CID is on the way, Sheila. The best you can do is run for it. Inez and I will promise not to say anything until you've had a chance to get away."

"You read too many novels, Mrs. Malloy," she said. Droplets of moisture splattered on my neck. "We're alone, and I'm getting bored. If you'll sit down on the bed—"

The light flashed on, harsh and unanticipated. My eyes saw nothing but great white circles that slowly dimmed to red as I blinked furiously. Sheila, on the other hand, must have seen the guns and scowls long before I did.

I was still blinking when she said, "Here, take it. I wasn't going to shoot anyone. I was just . . ."

Going to strangle them, I added silently. Lieutenant Rosen finally came into focus, his feral teeth adding to the glare. Sheila was whisked away by the omnipresent Jorgeson, no doubt to find herself in thumb screws on the petite rack. Inez was under the bed, whimpering. It was a good thing she hadn't had to fling herself into battle.

Minutes later, Inez was also whisked away to her mother's comforting bosom. That left me—and Sherlock.

By tacit agreement we went to the liquor cabinet in the living room. I poured a shy eight ounces of scotch, then went to the shrouded sofa and sat down. Lieutenant Rosen dug around until he found whiskey; I suspected the man was a barbarian the first time I heard his accent. Now it was confirmed.

"So you knew where Miss Brandon was hiding?" he said, watching the golden liquid slosh in his glass. It caught the light from the fixture above and glittered in a lazy whirlpool.

"I didn't know; I only wondered. It sccms I wondered well," I retorted. "If you had bothered to ask me at the cemetery, I would have told you. But Sherlock has to solve the case without any help from a mortal . . ." Thc scotch scalded my throat divinely, all the way from my tonsils to my toes.

"And the medallion?"

"How did you know that I—? Hendrix, right?"

He nodded and held out his hand. I found the thing in my pocket, tossed it in his direction, and sunk further into the shroud. "It was on poor Mildred's grave," I said. "Sheila must have carried it around in case she could use it to frame someone. Inez was the best she could find. That must have been a graver disappointment than the boudoir color scheme."

"Why give the medallion to Miss Brandon?"

"She must have felt the need to implicate Inez further. She followed her to the cemetery, offered the medallion, and then lured her here with some nonsense about rescuing Twilliam."

"Then tied up Miss Brandon and wafted into the shadows

to wait for you, Mrs. Malloy. Having made sure that you were aware of Caron's involvement, she knew you would come. Did it occur to you that you might have told me what you suspected?"

"And where is Twilliam, by the way?"

"Jorgeson's wife has filed adoption papers at the pound. Jorgeson has been mumbling about a barbecue; I think I'll pass up that invitation." He studied the medallion for a moment, then added, "You might have been eliminated, you know. The whole thing was arranged to ultimately get to you."

"Me? Mildred and Douglas would beg to differ, if they could," I retorted, trying not to squeak. "Why me?"

"Because of what your husband did to Sheila's sister eight years ago," Lieutenant Rosen said calmly, as if he hadn't mentioned my demise in an unnecessarily light tone. "Your husband had Sheila's sister with him when they had the wreck. Although the girl survived, she was terribly disfigured. She ended up in a nursing home, and three years ago she killed herself."

"Not Britton's girlfriend's sister?" I continued in the same shrill voice. Reality, where is thy volume control?

"She is thirteen years old. Farber wouldn't enroll her unless she had perfect SATs to go along with the tuition. And not even Douglas Twiller would mess with her—she has braces."

"You interviewed her? Braces and all?" It hadn't been a particularly good theory, but it had been my best. Some of it had been correct. Sheila, a sister with vengeance on her mind. All that effort, coming to Farber in the fine arts program, meeting Douglas and allowing him to seduce her, while stalking innocent little me all that time. The shudders got the best of me.

Before I could voice a protest, Lieutenant Rosen swooped down to grasp my shoulders. "Are you planning on hysterics? I suppose I ought to slap you or something."

"If you slap me, you'll eat cheek for a week," I said as I yanked myself free. Hysterics? A display of surprise, perhaps, and even a bit of disquiet. I do not have hysterics. Ever. I have scotch instead. I tossed off three inches in a discreet gulp.

The lieutenant edged out of range. "Is there anything else you'd like to know before we settle down to paperwork? The problem with the disappearing copies, anything at all?"

"No, thank you. I knew all the answers hours and hours ago. I just wanted to give the woman a chance to explain," I said haughtily.

"And shoot you," he agreed with his damned smile. His ego forced him to elaborate, since I didn't. "When her sister committed suicide, Miss Belinski swore revenge on the entire Farber faculty—and on you in particular. It took several years to put the plan in motion. She completed an undergraduate degree, applied to Farber, and was accepted in the graduate school. Between throwing pots she listened to campus gossip and learned that the Twillers were friends of yours. It was not difficult to wiggle her way into Twiller's bed, as countless coeds will attest. Pillow talk inspired the scheme. She readily supplied the information about your husband and his affair. I think she realized that you would not respond by going into seclusion to sulk."

"I do not sulk," I corrected him sulkily.

"In any case, she then perched on the edge of her web and watched. With Carlton, Caron, and Inez involved, she knew you'd trot into her parlor sooner or later. In the meantime, the faculty was indeed squirming over the book, which amused her no end."

"Why did Douglas agree to write the book?"

"Amiable Mr. Twiller had motives of his own. He had known for several months that his pen name was in jeopardy; if Mrs. Twiller actually refused to continue, he didn't particularly need her any longer."

"So he was willing to strangle her out of convenience?"

"In theory. A divorce would have hurt his chances for the promotion, and he would have been in no position to negotiate for the division of wealth. So he obediently wrote the book to Sheila's specifications, throwing in all kinds of nasty things about their cast of suspects. However, he backed out at the vital moment, and Sheila decided to see it through. Twiller was caught; he couldn't admit he was a part of the scheme to murder his wife."

"So he scurried off to bed with a new coed, just for appearances. I blabbed to Sheila, and then she killed him, too." I licked the rim of my empty glass. "My fault, I suppose."

Lieutenant Rosen shook his head to absolve me from the sin. "Twiller was waist-deep in it; he was at best an accessory to the murder of his wife, and he knew it. He just couldn't figure how to keep writing those trashy books without a front. The chairmanship of the English department would have eased his transition into the middle class."

"How did you and the Mounties manage to arrive at the crucial moment? Sheila had just announced she was getting bored when you stormed in. Ten seconds, and Inez and I would have been able to discuss the mess with Douglas and Mildred—in person."

"Caron called the police station. When you left the house on foot, she hung out the window long enough to see you reach the corner. Unfortunately, she couldn't tell which way you turned. We went by the Book Depot first."

"My daughter called you?"

"As any law-abiding citizen would do in the same situation."

I stared at him. "While you were fumbling around my bookstore, I might have been hurt. Of course, you should have known who was behind the scheme. Any detective worth his salary could have spotted the coincidence of the name and asked Sheila a few questions about her sister."

"Belinski came from a brief marriage. Her maiden name was Stephens, but nobody thought to ask. I should have realized that Twiller wasn't devious enough to pull off the murder; he couldn't carry on an affair without it being common knowledge on the campus. The only person who couldn't see through him was his wife."

"Poor old Douglas," I sighed. "I'm glad that he chickened out at the last moment."

We sat and sighed for a long time. Jorgeson came through at one point, gave us a curious look, and left the room. Hendrix even appeared briefly, looking much more palatable in a trim uniform and clean-shaven face.

I stuck out my hand. "You owe me five dollars."

Hendrix rummaged through his pocket and returned the bill. "I'm sorry about that, ma'am, but the lieutenant told me to watch out for a woman with red hair. He said she'd—" He halted, glanced in terror at Lieutenant Rosen, and backed out of the room, his mouth still open.

"Humph!" I snorted in the ensuing silence.

At last the lieutenant cleared his throat. "I seem to detect a certain emotional barrier between us, Mrs. Malloy."

"I just assumed we didn't much like each other, Lieutenant Rosen."

"Oh, really?" Insufferably egotistical.

"Ask your wife to explain it to you."

"I can't. My ex-wife lives in Montana and we communicate through lawyers. They'd never understand."

"Then it will remain a mystery, won't it?" I murmured, pleased with my nefarious ploy. "You may never understand why women don't fall into your arms whenever you crook your little finger."

"Why don't you let me run the investigation, for a change?"

It was time for a second drink. At the bar, I raised my eyebrows in response to the broad, pearly grin that shone across the room like the rising sun. I flashed all my teeth back at him.

"Have at it, Sherlock." He could think whatever he preferred. Who was I to meddle in a CID investigation?

About the Author

Joan Hess lives in Fayetteville, Arkansas. STRANGLED PROSE is her first novel

HODDER

A complete list of the FAMOUS FIVE ADVENTURES *by Enid Blyton*

---

1 FIVE ON A TREASURE ISLAND
2 FIVE GO ADVENTURING AGAIN
3 FIVE RUN AWAY TOGETHER
4 FIVE GO TO SMUGGLER'S TOP
5 FIVE GO OFF IN A CARAVAN
6 FIVE ON KIRRIN ISLAND AGAIN
7 FIVE GO OFF TO CAMP
8 FIVE GET INTO TROUBLE
9 FIVE FALL INTO ADVENTURE
10 FIVE ON A HIKE TOGETHER
11 FIVE HAVE A WONDERFUL TIME
12 FIVE GO DOWN TO THE SEA
13 FIVE GO TO MYSTERY MOOR
14 FIVE HAVE PLENTY OF FUN
15 FIVE ON A SECRET TRAIL
16 FIVE GO TO BILLYCOCK HILL
17 FIVE GET INTO A FIX
18 FIVE ON FINNISTON FARM
19 FIVE GO TO DEMON'S ROCKS
20 FIVE HAVE A MYSTERY TO SOLVE
21 FIVE ARE TOGETHER AGAIN

HODDER

A complete list of the SECRET SEVEN ADVENTURES *by Enid Blyton*

---

1 THE SECRET SEVEN
2 SECRET SEVEN ADVENTURE
3 WELL DONE, SECRET SEVEN
4 SECRET SEVEN ON THE TRAIL
5 GO AHEAD, SECRET SEVEN
6 GOOD WORK, SECRET SEVEN
7 SECRET SEVEN WIN THROUGH
8 THREE CHEERS, SECRET SEVEN
9 SECRET SEVEN MYSTERY
10 PUZZLE FOR THE SECRET SEVEN
11 SECRET SEVEN FIREWORKS
12 GOOD OLD SECRET SEVEN
13 SHOCK FOR THE SECRET SEVEN
14 LOOK OUT, SECRET SEVEN
15 FUN FOR THE SECRET SEVEN